Fortune's Children

Meet the Fortunes—three generations of a family with a legacy of wealth, influence and power. As they gather for a host of weddings, passionate new romances are ignited…and shocking family secrets are revealed…

RENEE RILEY: This dutiful daughter was all set to marry Mr Wrong to save her family's business until she found herself secluded in a remote hideaway with Mr Right!

GARRETT FORTUNE: This stubborn man had learned that most women only wanted one thing from him—his money. But Renee Riley *seemed* different. Could he really trust her?

KATE FORTUNE: The indomitable, forever-young family matriarch is at it again!

Meanwhile…

JACK FORTUNE: Garrett's brother has just become a single dad. Will his unexpected new role force this powerful tycoon to see what—and who—is right under his nose?

Fortune Family Tree

Caleb Fortune* m. Lilah Dulaine

Stuart Fortune m. Marie Smith

Emmet Fortune m. Annie Mackenzie (d)

② GARRETT Fortune
--m.--
Renee Riley

③ JACK Fortune
--1st m.--
Sandra Alexander (d)
--b--
Lily Fortune

④ MOLLIE SHAW**

① MACKENZIE Fortune
--m.--
Kelly Sinclair

Chad Fortune

⑤ CHLOE Fortune

Key:
① The Honour-Bound Groom
② Society Bride
③ The Secretary and the Millionaire
④ The Groom's Revenge
⑤ Undercover Groom

Symbols:

- - - - -   Affair

{   Twins

*   Kate Fortune's brother-in-law

**   Child of Affair

Fortune's Children™

BRIDES

SOCIETY BRIDE
Elizabeth Bevarly

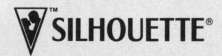

™ SILHOUETTE®

*First published in Great Britain 2000
Silhouette Books, Eton House, 18-24 Paradise Road,
Richmond, Surrey TW9 1SR*

© Harlequin Books S.A. 1999

Special thanks and acknowledgement to
Elizabeth Bevarly for her contribution to the
FORTUNE'S CHILDREN: THE BRIDES series.

ISBN 0 373 76196 1

26-0005

*Printed and bound in Spain
by Litografia Rosés S.A., Barcelona*

For my editor, Gail Chasan,
who takes very, very good care of me.
Thank you.

And with many thanks to Dan(ny) Bevarly and Carl
Brazley of Mo'Better Marketing, who really came
through in a pinch. I owe you guys big.

ELIZABETH BEVARLY

is an honours graduate of the University of Louisville
and achieved her dream of writing full-time before she
even turned thirty! At heart, she is also an avid voyager
who once helped navigate a friend's thirty-five-foot
sailboat across the Bermuda Triangle. 'I really love to
travel,' says this self-avowed beach bum. 'To me, it's the
best education a person can give to herself.' Her dream
is to one day have her own sailboat, a beautifully
renovated older-model forty-two-footer, and to enjoy
the freedom and tranquillity seafaring can bring.
Elizabeth likes to think she has a lot in common with
the characters she creates—people who know love and
life go hand in hand. And she's getting some first-hand
experience with motherhood, as well—she and her
husband have a four-year-old son, Eli.

Silhouette® is proud to present

**Meet the Fortune brides: special women
who perpetuate a family legacy greater
than mere riches!**

April 2000
A FORTUNE'S CHILDREN WEDDING:
THE HOODWINKED BRIDE
Barbara Boswell

THE HONOUR-BOUND GROOM
Jennifer Greene

May 2000
SOCIETY BRIDE
Elizabeth Bevarly

THE SECRETARY AND THE MILLIONAIRE
Leanne Banks

June 2000
THE GROOM'S REVENGE
Susan Crosby

UNDERCOVER GROOM
Merline Lovelace

**Remember, where there's a bride…
there's a _wedding!_**

One

"**B**ut, Daddy, I barely *know* him. How can you ask me to do something like…like *that* with him?"

Renee Riley chewed anxiously on her thumbnail and stared dumbfounded at her father in light of what he'd just asked her to do. Then she remembered that one of her New Year's resolutions was to stop biting her fingernails— Hey, so what if it was only New Year's Eve? No time like the present, right?—and she forced her hand to her side. Unable to keep still, however, she immediately lifted it again, this time to run her fingers through her curly, chin-length, dark brown hair.

All around her was music and laughter and joyful noise, and it struck her as ironic that she would be standing in the middle of a wedding reception—and playing the role of maid of honor, too—pondering the request her father had just made of her. Another ripple of distaste rolled through her, making her queasy, and her fist tightened around the bouquet of red roses and baby's breath nestled against the sleeveless burgundy velvet sheath she wore.

"Renee, sweetheart," Reginald Riley pleaded in that cajoling tone that had always been her undoing, "what Lyle Norton wants to do isn't so surprising. You're a beautiful girl, after all, and he's a young, red-blooded man, so naturally he'd want you to—"

"But, Daddy," Renee interrupted him, something she normally never did. Which just went to show how very desperate she was. "It's such a…such an *intimate* thing to do. I mean, how can Mr. Norton ask someone he hardly knows to… How can *you* ask *me* to—"

"Oh, come on, Renee." Reginald interrupted her. "Be reasonable. It's not like I'm asking you to sleep with him."

She narrowed her eyes. "Daddy, you've just told me that a man I barely know wants to marry me, and you approve of the idea. Now, aside from the fact that this whole thing is totally archaic—a fact upon which I won't *even* comment at length right now—hasn't it occurred to you that, if I do marry Mr. Norton, then at some point, sleeping with him is going to figure into the deal?"

Her father furrowed his brows thoughtfully. "Oh," he replied blandly, as if that particular part of the arrangement hadn't quite jelled in his brain. "Oh, yeah. Then I, uh, I guess I am asking you to sleep with him. But only under the sanctity of marriage." He hastened to qualify his words, as if that made everything perfectly okeydoke.

Oh, well, gee, Renee thought, *in that case…*

"And you talk like the two of you are strangers, honey," he continued. "And that's just not true."

"Showing up at three parties where he also happened to be a guest does *not* a relationship make," she told him.

"Hey, your mother and I got engaged the *second* time we saw each other," Reginald reminded her.

"Oh, sure, the night before you boarded a plane for Vietnam," Renee reminded him. "There was an element of urgency there that isn't exactly consistent with this situation. Besides, you always said it was love at first sight with you and Mama."

"And you don't think you could love Lyle?"

Renee hunched her shoulders uncomfortably and didn't answer straight out. Instead, she said, very quietly, "Daddy...he's your business rival."

Her father made a face, as if he really hadn't wanted to be reminded of that particular fact. To counter his sour expression, he said, just as softly, "He's only doing his job."

She managed a chuckle at that, but there wasn't an ounce of good humor in the sound. "His job is corporate raider," she pointed out unnecessarily. "His whole reason for existence is to take advantage of failing companies and consume them in one big bite."

Her father nodded disconsolately. "And now he's going after Riley Communications because it's one of those failing businesses. I know."

"So how can you ask me to marry a man who would snatch your livelihood right out from under you?"

He sighed resolutely. "Because, Renee, it's the only way to save the company."

She narrowed her eyes. "What do you mean?"

Reginald inhaled deeply and took her hand in his, meeting her gaze levelly. "Look, I'll be honest with you," he said. "Lyle has told me in no uncertain terms that he'll make a deal with me that would insure I keep the company and receive all the funds necessary to bring it back into the black."

Oh, she wasn't going to like this. Renee could tell already. In spite of that, she said, "Go on."

"Lyle has flat-out told me that if you'll marry him, he'll release his grip on Riley Communications, and instead of taking it away from me—from us—he'll leave it in my hands *and* invest a substantial amount of money to turn things around. We're talking millions of dollars, Renee, money that I simply do not have. To put it in mercenary terms, sweetheart, for the price of your hand in marriage, you and I get to keep Riley Communications. It's that simple."

"What?" she demanded. "Daddy, this is like something out of the Middle Ages."

"Not necessarily," he told her. But, deep down, he seemed no more convinced of that than she. "Marriages of convenience still take place in this day and age. Precisely for reasons like this—economics. It's not so unusual."

"But…" She sighed heavily. "Daddy, how can I possibly marry him? I hardly know him, let alone love him. And marriage…that's for life."

He hesitated as if struggling to phrase his next words. His gaze never faltered from hers as he told her, "Lyle Norton is a man who could have anything—anyone—he wants, Renee. But he's also a busy man, one whose working schedule prohibits him from socializing much. He simply does not have many opportunities to meet women on other than a business level, and those he does meet don't have the qualifications he requires in a wife."

Before Renee had a chance to comment, her father hurried on. "And on those few occasions when he's met you, he's been very taken with you. He thinks you would be the perfect wife for him. Then again," he continued with a halfhearted smile, "why wouldn't he want the best, right?"

"But why does he think *I'd* be the perfect wife?" Renee asked, wondering why she was continuing this conversation when what her father had proposed was totally unthinkable. "He and I have engaged in *maybe* three conversations total."

Her father smiled. "Lyle told me that your presence by his side would be the perfect complement to his life-style and his plans for the future. You're beautiful, educated, socially prominent…"

"Thrifty, kind, obedient, trustworthy," Renee muttered under her breath. In other words, she thought dryly, to Lyle Norton, she would be an accessory right up there with a solid gold money clip. "I think Mr. Norton might do better with a golden retriever," she added softly.

"What?" her father asked.

"Nothing."

"He does seem to be genuinely taken with you, Renee," Reginald continued, "even if the two of you aren't well acquainted. And even I, on the receiving end of his—'' he hesitated, then evidently decided to call a spade a spade ''—his ruthless, blindly ambitious business practices...will concede that he's what might be considered quite a catch. Any other girl in Minneapolis would probably be shopping for a wedding gown right now.''

Renee smiled sadly. ''Nice try, Daddy. But I still think this whole thing is crazy.''

He nodded resolutely. ''Look, I can't force you to marry him,'' her father said. ''But with the way things stand right now, honey, we're going to lose everything. Everything. Not just the company, but the house, the cars, your mother's jewelry...''

''Mama's jewelry?'' she echoed. ''But—''

But Mama's jewelry wasn't even worth that much, Renee thought. Except for its sentimental value, which, to her at least, made it priceless.

''I've made a mess of things, sweetheart,'' Reginald admitted. ''While you were away at college, I took some chances, made some bad investments.'' He shrugged sadly. ''I've compromised everything I tried to build up for you and future generations of Rileys. It'll be gone.'' He snapped his fingers. ''Like that. All those years of hard work and sacrifice for nothing. And, frankly, I don't know what I'll do if I lose it.''

Something cold and sharp twisted deep inside Renee to see her father like this. He'd always stood so proud and tall, had always had so many plans for the future. He'd started off with nothing, driven to escape the poverty he'd grown up in, he'd dedicated his entire life to building Riley Communications into a rousing, enormous success.

What had made his feat doubly impressive was that he'd done it as a single father after Renee's mother died when she was two. Reginald had devoted every moment that wasn't given to the company to making sure his daughter's life was as happy and full as it could possibly be. And when he couldn't spend time on her, he spent money, indulging her every whim, spoiling and pampering her, more, really, than was necessary.

But he did so because he loved her. Because he wanted to be certain she never experienced the pain and hunger he'd known as a boy. And because of the time they'd spent together and the highs and lows they'd shared, the two of them had forged a stronger father-daughter bond than most families claimed.

Her father would do anything for her, Renee knew. And he had made so many sacrifices over the years to insure her happiness. So how come she was balking at doing something that might repay him for all the things he'd done for her?

Really, Lyle Norton wasn't that bad, she had to admit. Everybody else in Minneapolis thought he was just about the best thing to come along since Belgian chocolate. He had come out of nowhere five years ago to become the talk—and the toast— of the local business community. Phrases like "boy wonder" and "golden boy" were frequently tossed about to describe him, and he was always the centerpiece of every event he attended.

He seemed like a nice enough guy. And he was handsome. And charming. And articulate. Polite, too. All in all, Lyle Norton was pretty much perfect. In fact, when she got right down to it, she had to concede that Lyle Norton was so utterly lacking in flaws, so absolutely perfect that...

Well, there were times when he gave Renee the creeps. He was, in her opinion, at least—she might as well just say it— plastic and smarmy and ingratiating. Worse than all those things, though, he seemed to have no sense of humor at all. The only time she'd seen the man smile was when he heard about a rise in the stock market or the failure of a business he wanted for his own. Nothing else in life seemed to bring Lyle Norton pleasure.

Except, evidently, the prospect of marrying Reginald Riley's only daughter.

"I hate to ask you to even consider this, Renee," her father said, jarring her from her musing. "But you're our only

chance to hang on to the company, to hang on to the very life-
style that we have. If you don't marry him, we'll lose everything.''

When she said nothing, he added, ''At least consider it,
sweetheart. Thinking you don't know Lyle well enough is
something that's easily rectified. Just make it a long engagement. Take your time getting to know him. You might discover that you really like him. You could even fall in love
with him—you never know. And he'd be a good provider.
You'd never lack for anything.''

No, she'd certainly never lack for anything, Renee thought.
Except maybe for love. Except maybe for that heady, dizzying
sensation that turns a person upside down and inside out, never
knowing for sure if it's day or night, and frankly never caring.

Oh, but, hey, other than that…

Not that Renee had ever experienced such a sensation. To
be honest, she wasn't convinced such an emotion even existed.
Although she was only twenty-three, she'd never come close
to falling in love. In fact, the whole starry-eyed, hot-summer-
night romance thing eluded her. Her friends who had succumbed to what they called love had generally wound up making fools of themselves at best or suffering the depths of de-
spair at worst. So it could be that lacking love in a relationship
might wind up being a *good* thing in the long run.

And it wasn't that she *dis*liked Mr. Norton. On the contrary,
in spite of his smarminess and ingratiating tactics, she had no
choice but to admire him for becoming the massive success
he was at such an early age. At twenty-six, he was only three
years older than she, yet he'd accomplished infinitely more
than she had. In fact, he'd made his first million when he was
twenty-three. Renee didn't even have a job. And in a few short
years, Lyle had gone on to build a corporate empire that
wouldn't be easily toppled. Renee, if she was lucky, might be
doing something by the time she was twenty-six that wasn't
immersing frozen French fries into a deep-fat pit.

Of course, she knew she shouldn't sell herself short. She
had, after all, just earned her MA in liberal arts. And along

with her BA in humanities, that was going to make her perfectly suited to—to…

Well, now that Renee thought about it, there wasn't a whole lot she *would* be suited to. Except, perhaps—thanks to all those years of etiquette schooling—being a first-rate hostess and a fine conversationalist. Which, now that she thought *more* about it, might be exactly the kind of training she needed to be a corporate wife to someone like, oh, say…Lyle Norton.

So what if he didn't wreak havoc with her heart? The least Renee could do was *try* to get to know him better and *consider* the man's proposal.

Hey, as her father just said, he was quite a catch, a man who would take good care of Renee—financially, at least. She supposed, to her father, that was the most important thing. Always the businessman—that was her dad. As much as she knew he loved her, he would be just as concerned about making sure she was provided for economically as cared for emotionally.

Then again, maybe there was something to be said for that, too.…

Renee sighed fitfully as she ran her hand through her hair again. It had been a long day, and her maid of honor duties had left her feeling too tired to argue. So she glanced down, caressing the delicate red blooms of her bouquet instead of meeting her father's gaze. And quietly, reluctantly, she said, "Okay, Daddy. I'll consider everything you've said. I'll think about marrying Lyle Norton."

And she would, too, she promised herself as her father kissed her on the cheek and made his way into the crowd of celebratory guests at her friend Kelly Sinclair's wedding. She'd think about it very seriously. But not here. Not where Kelly had just marked the beginning of a union with her new husband, Mac Fortune, and the baby they were expecting next month. Not where there was so much warmth and promise of good things to come.

Renee glanced toward the floor-to-ceiling windows in the conference room of the Fortune Corporation, a conference room that had been transformed for the ceremony, thanks to a miracle-worker wedding planner. A red velvet carpet eclipsed the floor, satin ribbons hung from the sides of the conference chairs, and at the front of the room, the dais was nearly obscured by pots and sprays of flowers—delicate baby's breath, red, red roses and sweet-smelling gardenias. The lighting was soft and buttery, the music muted and joyful.

And outside, as if cued to do so, snow fell in a flurry of fat, furious flakes, turning the night sky into a magical sight. Something about the dreamy dance of white satin snow against the black velvet backdrop made Renee smile. Snow buffed all the hard edges from everything, softened whatever it touched, made beautiful what might otherwise be an ugly scene. Snow was quiet. Peaceful. Soothing. Sneaking outside to watch the snow fall, she thought, might help to clear her head.

The wedding party was small—no more than thirty people—so she figured she could slip out unobserved. Kelly and Mac, the newlyweds, were still mingling, and because it was New Year's Eve, no one seemed anxious to get home.

Renee saw her father engaged in what appeared to be a *very* intense conversation with Stuart Fortune, and she knew it would be a while before he felt like leaving. So, confident that she could steal away without being missed, she eased out the conference room door.

For a long time, she simply sat in Kelly's office gazing out the window at the snow. She thought about how she and Kelly had become fast friends in Girl Scouts so many years ago, about Lyle Norton and about her father's hard work. She even tried to recall snippets of memories about her mother. But mostly, Renee thought about love. About whether or not it really existed, about the different forms it might take. And she wondered…

Well, she wondered about a lot of things.

And she began to grow restless.

She'd been in the Fortune Building often enough with Kelly that she knew her way around fairly well. At the end of the corridor outside was a small terrace that offered a spectacular

view of the Minneapolis skyline. She and Kelly had met there
to share lunch on a number of occasions, along with a handful
of other employees who brown-bagged it. It was the perfect
place to which to retreat while pondering the dilemma her
father had posed.

So she donned the ivory cashmere coat she'd left in Kelly's
office earlier. There was nothing she could do about her shoes,
but the high-heeled pumps would keep her feet warm enough
for the little time she would be alone outside.

However, she discovered as she stepped through the sliding
glass doors that led to the terrace, she wouldn't be alone outside. Protected from the snow by a generous overhang, a tall,
dark figure leaned against the bricks not ten feet away from
her, one knee bent, his foot braced against the wall behind
him. He had one hand curved under the bowl of a champagne
flute that was filled nearly to the brim with bubbly golden
wine, the other shoved deep into his trouser pocket. His head
was tipped back, and he was staring at the sky, but he didn't
seem to be seeing much of anything.

Garrett Fortune, she realized. Mac's best man. She'd barely
exchanged a dozen words with him, but the sight of him standing there alone, a tall, dark silhouette against a swirl of white,
ignited a spark of heat inside her that quickly blossomed into
a near forest fire. She didn't know why he should wreak such
havoc with her senses. But all through the rehearsal last night
and all during the wedding this evening, Renee's every instinct
had homed in on him as if he were a beacon of salvation in
the blackest night.

And although he had barely acknowledged her, there had
been moments when she'd caught him eyeing her in a way
that left her feeling oddly flustered. Bereft. Hot. The man
roused a yearning inside her unlike anything she'd felt before.

It was the strangest thing. Renee had never *yearned* for anything before. Wanted, yes. Desired, certainly. But this yearning
business was something completely different. Before, whenever she'd wanted or desired, her father had made sure she
got whatever was necessary to fulfill her, or Renee went about

achieving fulfillment for herself. But something told her this yearning she felt every time she came within twenty feet of Garrett Fortune wouldn't be so easy to satisfy.

"Hi." Renee greeted him, trying to be friendly. After all, they would be sharing a terrace.

He started, snapping his head around to look at her. His stiff stance eased when he saw who had hailed him, but he still appeared wary.

Strange, Renee thought. Usually it was the woman alone at night who claimed the right to feel cautious when confronted by the opposite sex. Somehow, though, she wasn't the least bit threatened by Garrett. On the contrary, she sensed a wall of defense surrounding the guy.

"Hi, yourself," he replied. His voice was deep, smooth, warm, reminding Renee of a generous shot of cognac—old cognac, the kind that went down oh, so smoothly and heated you up from the inside out.

In spite of that, she shoved her hands deep into her coat pockets. "The snow is beautiful, isn't it?" she asked, taking a few steps toward him.

He stared at the fat flakes plummeting down, and for the first time, she noted that he wasn't wearing a coat. Just a dark, clearly very expensive suit, a crisp white dress shirt and a night-colored tie. In spite of the freezing temperatures—or perhaps in defiance of them—he'd loosened that tie, and had unfastened the top button of his shirt. Somehow she got the impression that being comfortable was infinitely more important to him than being exposed to the elements.

Then again, those elements seemed to be almost inherent in his nature. As warm as he made her feel inside, his reception to her was a bit chilly.

"Beauty can be deceiving," he said, turning toward her. "This is supposed to turn into a full-force blizzard before the night is over. In this case, beauty can be downright dangerous."

When he turned, his face was thrown into the light tumbling from a nearby window, and Renee noticed again what an exceedingly handsome man he was. He was quite a bit older than she—probably in his mid-thirties. The light gilded his light brown hair—hair that was longer than one might expect on a man suited to suits. His eyes were pale brown, and his mouth...

She bit back a sigh, as she always did when her gaze settled inevitably on Garrett's mouth. His mouth was at once soft and fierce, inviting and wary, luscious and forbidding. Much like the man himself, she thought.

She shrugged. "There's no reason you can't enjoy it now, though," she said, clutching her coat more tightly around her. "Seems harmless enough for the time being."

"The operative word here being 'seems,'" he said.

She smiled. "Or maybe the operative words would be 'for the time being.'"

"Or maybe it's the 'harmless' part I should be worrying about," he said. "Maybe that's what's really so deceiving."

Renee eyed him thoughtfully. "Something tells me we're having two totally different conversations here."

He chuckled, but the sound was less than happy. "Yeah. Story of my life."

The moment he uttered the words, Garrett Fortune realized they were stained with bitterness. And his new companion noticed, too, because her smile—a smile that had nearly blinded him, so dazzling had it been—immediately fell. And when it did, suddenly, somehow, he felt as if a door slammed shut deep inside his soul.

Man, his emotions must be rubbed raw tonight if he was reacting like this to a woman like Renee Riley. Oh, sure, she was cute and everything, even seemed kind of sweet, from what he'd seen of her at last night's rehearsal and tonight's wedding. But harmless? Not bloody likely. Not to him. She was exactly the kind of woman he knew to avoid.

God, he hated weddings. Why hadn't he made up some lame excuse to give Mac—like he was bleeding from a mortal wound or something—and just stayed home?

His cool reception didn't deter Renee. She covered the distance between them in a half-dozen easy strides. Then she took up a place beside him at the wall, adopting a stance much like his. Well, except that her stance was nearly a foot shorter than his, and she probably weighed a good hundred pounds less.

Garrett fought back a smile at the sight of her and enjoyed an idle sip of his champagne. He frowned when he noted her attire. Of course, she *was* the maid of honor, he reminded himself. But the least she could have done was put on a decent pair of shoes before coming out in the cold. The snow was only a few inches deep on the terrace, but it easily brushed her feet where her shoes ended and her stockings began. At this rate, she'd be taking home frostbite as a wedding favor.

Dim debutante, he thought. Then again, at least she was wearing a coat, which was more than he could say for *some* people standing on this terrace. But he was bad-tempered and self-destructive, right? Everybody said so. He was entitled.

"So…what did you think of the wedding?" she asked, clearly striving to end what was fast becoming an awkward moment.

Relieved at the introduction of small talk, Garrett took another sip of his wine. "I thought the wedding was beautiful," he said amiably, "especially for one thrown together so quickly."

"Yeah, me, too," she agreed as she hugged her coat to herself again. "Mollie did a wonderful job. Of course, she's a friend of Kelly's so I'm sure she added a lot of extra special touches."

"And I also think marriage is a complete waste of time and a total farce," Garrett added as if she hadn't spoken. Funny, he wasn't sure when, exactly, he'd decided to say such a thing aloud.

His companion blinked in surprise at his announcement before expelling a soft sound of disbelief. "Well, gosh, don't hide your feelings," she said dryly. "If you want to voice an opinion, just spit it out."

He smiled at that, then uttered another rough chuckle.

"Sorry," he replied, even though he felt not one iota of regret. "That just kind of popped out."

"Yeah, I'll say it did."

He sighed and turned, leaning his shoulder against the wall so that he could observe her more intently. She was young, probably still in college. Pretty, though, in an uptown-girl kind of way. Dark curls tumbled riotously about her face, falling low over pale green eyes encircled by long, sooty lashes. The cold air had stained her cheeks with red, and her lips... He bit back a restless sound. Her lips, too, were touched with crimson, though whether the color resulted from cosmetics or the cold, he honestly couldn't have said.

If he kissed her, he bet he could find out for sure.

Startled by the thought, Garrett pushed it away and forced himself to focus on the conversation at hand.

"I've just seen too many people get married for the wrong reasons, that's all," he said by way of an explanation. "Then things start going bad, and a messy divorce clinches all the nasty feelings."

"Gee, you sound like you're speaking from experience," Renee said quietly.

For a moment, he wondered where she got off making such a personal observation about someone she barely knew. Then he realized that he'd been the one to start it. He had no one to blame but himself.

So he replied frankly. "Maybe that's because I am."

Renee eyed him thoughtfully for a moment, but instead of pursuing his confession, she asked, "Are you suggesting that Kelly and Mac married for the wrong reasons?"

Garrett shrugged. "Well, it's not exactly a love match when a man marries a woman who got herself knocked up by his little brother, is it?"

"Excuse me," she said indignantly, quick to jump to her friend's defense, "but a woman doesn't get herself pregnant all alone, you know. Chad Fortune—that jerk—had a little something to do with the whole thing."

Garrett expelled an impatient sigh. "Yeah, and now Mac is the one paying for it."

"You make it sound like he was forced to marry Kelly against his will."

"Wasn't he?"

"Of course not. He was the one who made the offer."

"And she was the one who jumped at the chance to be a Fortune wife."

"Oh, come on," Renee said, straightening to her full height of what couldn't possibly be more than five feet four inches, clearly spoiling for a fight.

Garrett smiled the most predatory smile he could summon and straightened to his own six-feet-plus, fully ready to take her on.

But she didn't back down. "The baby that Kelly is carrying is a Fortune. Why should she deny the little nipper its birthright?"

"Its birthright is *Chad* Fortune, not Mac," Garrett pointed out. "But Chad's always been good at leaving a mess for Mac to clean up."

"A mess?" she echoed incredulously. "That's what you call a pregnant woman who's been abandoned by the baby's father? A pregnant woman who was recently *attacked,* by unknown assailants, no less, and needs someone to keep an eye on her now? You think that's a *mess?*"

He frowned. "You know what I meant."

She nodded. "Yeah, unfortunately I do. You're one of those snotty rich guys who think the only thing women want out of them is their money, and that said women will stop at nothing to get it. You never look at the big picture."

"And you," he countered, hating himself for rising so quickly to the bait, even if what she said did cut way too close to home, "are doubtless one of those greedy opportunists who think snagging a rich husband will insure a cushy life of ease where she'll never have to lift a finger."

She gaped at him, as if she were trying to decide whether to defend herself or return to defending her friend. Ultimately, gallantly, she chose the latter. "I think you're wrong about Mac and Kelly. I think they make a good match."

"They don't love each other," Garrett said.

She seemed to think seriously for a moment before replying, "Maybe, in the long run, that will make things easier for them. Maybe not having love in their relationship will make their union stronger."

He narrowed his eyes. "Funny, but somehow, I had you pegged as the more romantic type. Hearts and flowers and love forever after. All that mushy stuff."

She dropped her gaze to the ground. "Yeah, well, maybe you had me pegged wrong. Just because they didn't marry for love doesn't mean the commitment between Mac and Kelly isn't strong. They had more to think about than love. They have a responsibility and obligation to an unborn child."

She seemed struck by her own comment and lapsed into a thoughtful silence for another moment before continuing in a voice of enlightenment, "In fact, maybe it's *commitment* that's really *most* important in a marriage, you know? Not love, not passion but…responsibility. Obligation. Doing the right thing, I mean."

"Gee, keep saying it over and over like that, and maybe eventually you'll start to believe it," Garrett said wryly, wondering why she was trying to convince herself of something even he could see she didn't truly believe.

"No, really," she insisted, glancing up. But she focused on something over his left shoulder and didn't quite meet his eyes. "For centuries, marriage was used to fatten family fortunes and further political ambitions. Love never figured into it at all. And a lot of those marriages were probably just as enduring as the ones founded on love—more enduring, even. Today, still, there are probably lots of people who get married for reasons other than love."

"Gee, you really think so?" Garrett asked dryly, knowing she didn't think it for a moment. In spite of his conviction, however, she nodded vigorously. A little *too* vigorously, he thought.

"Yeah," she said halfheartedly. "Probably."

He nodded, too, deciding that if Renee Riley wanted to live in a world where obligation and responsibility were more important than romantic love, he sure as hell wasn't going to dissuade her of the notion. Why should he, when he was of exactly the same opinion?

Still, for some reason, it bothered him to see a kid like her being jaded so young—especially when she probably hadn't had a chance yet to be beaten down by life. Because everybody should get beaten down by life once in a while, right? What would be the fun otherwise? Sheesh.

Naturally, Garrett's jadedness came from experience. He'd graduated at the top of his class from the school of hard knocks, by God, and he wore his diploma around his neck where *everybody* could see it. At this point in her life, Renee Riley wouldn't even qualify for a partial scholarship to his alma mater. She was just too ingenuous-looking, too fresh, too seemingly nice a kid. And he found himself wondering what on earth had made her lose her romanticism so early on.

Ah, well. None of his business. He'd never see her again after tonight. So if she wanted to think there was a hope in hell of Kelly and Mac living happily ever after just because they'd made a commitment to each other, then Garrett didn't see the harm.

She leaned against the wall and stared into space, as if she were giving serious thought to a matter that might have global repercussions. Garrett was about to say something that might alleviate the heaviness of the mood when, below them, the city erupted in celebration. Car horns blared, people shouted, and faintly, from somewhere far off, the soft strains of "Auld Lang Syne" crept through the stillness of the cold night air.

"Must be midnight," he said, removing his hand from his pocket to verify his assumption with a glance at his watch. Sure enough, the second hand was just leaving the other two, which remained perched at twelve o'clock. "To the new year," he added.

He smiled at Renee and lifted his half-full glass of champagne in a toast before moving it to his lips for a celebratory sip. As he lowered it, he realized she had nothing with which to welcome in the new year, so he extended the glass toward her in a silent offer.

After a moment's hesitation and a brief shrug, she accepted it, tipping it toward her mouth—that red, ripe, luscious mouth—to enjoy a taste of the wine. After a single quick sip, she lifted it a second time, filling her mouth more generously. When she held the glass out to Garrett, he noted a perfect crescent-shaped stain of red on the rim where her lips had been. And deep down inside him, something tightened, raw and fierce.

"Happy New Year, Renee," he said quietly, smiling as he took the glass from her fingers.

She smiled back. "Happy New Year, Garrett."

And then, because she seemed to expect more—or, perhaps, because he wanted more—he dipped his head and touched his lips to hers.

Just like that.

One little kiss, he told himself. Just a brief brush of his mouth over hers, to see if her lips were as soft and warm as they appeared to be. But, too late, he realized a single, idle caress was in no way enough to satisfy what suddenly became a deep hunger for the closeness of another human being. So instead of pulling away, Garrett took a step toward her, circling one arm around her waist to draw her closer still, at once fearful and hopeful that she would push him away.

But she didn't push him away.

Although she pulled her head back for a moment, fixing her gaze on his in a silent question, she neither said nor did anything to discourage him. On the contrary, she opened one hand over his chest and curled her fingers into his lapel, as if she wanted to pull him closer. So Garrett lowered his head to kiss her once more. He brushed his mouth lightly over hers once, twice, three times, breathless, brief little kisses that meant nothing, nothing at all.

Not until Renee kissed him back.

Kissed him back with a tentative, teasing touch that unleashed something deep down inside him that galloped quickly to the surface and made him hungry for more. So, without thinking about what he was doing, Garrett tightened his hold on Renee and pressed his mouth more possessively over hers, covering it, filling it, plundering it.

For a moment, she went limp in his arms, completely surrendering to his raw invasion. Then, just when he thought she would join in the fun, she jerked her mouth from his and hastily pushed him away. "I have to go," she said raggedly, avoiding his eyes. "I've been gone a long time. My father must be waiting for me, worried about me." And then, without a further word—or even a glance over her shoulder—she was gone.

As he watched her disappear through the sliding glass doors on the other side of the terrace, Garrett stood silent amid a swirl of snow, wondering what the hell had just happened.

Helplessly, he lifted a hand to his mouth and brushed his fingertips lightly over the lips Renee Riley had warmed with her mouth. Then he gazed at the perfect red stain of lipstick on his champagne flute. Without questioning his motives—or his sanity, for that matter—he turned the glass to place his own mouth over exactly that same spot and downed the rest of its contents in one long swallow.

And he decided that, as new years went, this one wasn't starting off well at all.

Two

The first week in April found Renee Riley feeling confused, agitated, anxious and seriously questioning her choice of a wedding dress. Because the one she'd selected for her impending—or rather *upcoming,* she hastily corrected herself— wedding to Lyle Norton suddenly seemed somewhat…inappropriate.

It had been created from roughly a bazillion yards of delicate white lace and was decorated with hundreds of seed pearls and scores of tiny white satin roses. Its train went on for all eternity, making it the perfect dress for a bride who was giddy with joy and anticipation at the prospect of joining herself to a man with whom she was deeply and irrevocably in love.

In other words, it wasn't Renee's cup of tea at all.

She sighed heavily as she gazed at her reflection in the cheval mirror that mocked her from the corner of her bedroom. For perhaps the twentieth time since she'd picked up the dress from the seamstress that morning, she held it up before her and swallowed hard against the nausea that rolled through her stomach. Her wedding was barely a week away, and Renee still couldn't quite remember how she'd agreed to the arrangement. Especially since it had been barely three months since Lyle—at least she had managed to finally stop calling him *Mr. Norton*—had approached her father about the merger.

Union, she corrected herself. What she and Lyle were undertaking was a union, not a merger. And her wedding was upcoming, not impending. Goodness, she was going to have to work on her semantics if she had any hope of making this farce—or rather, endeavor—succeed.

Her groom, naturally, was experiencing none of her misgivings. Of course, he'd been so busy with work lately that he'd scarcely been around for any of the wedding preparations. Nevertheless, he was delighted at the prospect of his and Renee's impending—*upcoming,* she reminded herself again—nuptials.

She expelled another heavy sigh as she folded the dress in half, held it away and gazed at her reflection without the garment. She looked pale with fatigue. She looked worried. She looked scared. Doubtless because she *was* all of those things.

So much for her father's suggestion that she and Lyle make it a long engagement so she could get to know her prospective husband better. Somehow—Renee was still at a loss as to *quite* how—Lyle had talked her into scheduling the wedding for the second weekend in April. It was, he'd told her, the best time for him, businesswise, because the rest of his year was booked solid with professional obligations. But Renee had hardly seen him during those three all-too-brief months, because that time had been booked solid with professional obligations, too.

And even on those few occasions when they *had* managed to find time together, Lyle was frequently called away early to attend to—what else?—professional obligations. As a result, she'd found herself feeling about as familiar and as comfortable with her husband-to-be as she would feel explaining the particulars of quantum physics.

She was also having serious second thoughts about this whole fiasco—or rather, marriage. Yes, she and Lyle did get along fine, even if they had yet to share much more than a few less-than-explosive kisses. And yes, her father was delighted at the prospect of hanging on to Riley Communications, Inc. And yes, Renee's future did look bright and promising to any casual observer, even if, to her, it was a tad lacking in, oh…life.

She should be happy, she told herself. She was engaged to a handsome, successful man who seemed to care for her, even if he wasn't exactly the passionate, cherish-is-the-word sort of mate that most women—other women, women who *weren't* Renee Riley—dreamed about.

She and Lyle were compatible, she reminded herself. They'd agreed on nearly everything they'd discussed—though they had yet to discuss much at any great depth. Still, they were able to carry on conversations that, if not exactly impassioned and important, were lively and interesting. Well, sort of lively, anyway. Sort of interesting.

And who needed romance, huh? Not her. No way. Why spend the rest of her life searching for something that probably didn't exist anyway, and even if it *did* exist, probably didn't live up to what everybody made it out to be.

If she passed up this chance with Lyle, she might never find another man who suited her. She might wind up utterly and totally alone. She might die a virgin—not that she really wanted to think too much about sex where Lyle was concerned, not until she had to. And as if all that weren't enough, she would end up a shriveled, bad-tempered old maid, *and* she still would have caused her father to lose Riley Communications in the process. Who needed to take a chance like that? Not Renee. Uh-uh. No, sir.

Really, she thought, she wasn't likely to do better for herself than Lyle. She was the envy of several—well, at least two— of her friends. Hey, she was probably—no, *certainly*—the envy of the majority of young women in Minneapolis. She was lucky to have Lyle. He was a wonderful man. Her life with him was bound to be really, truly very…good.

Gee, keeping saying it over and over like that, and maybe eventually you'll start to believe it.

Garrett Fortune's words haunted Renee, just as they'd haunted her repeatedly over the past three months. Just as Garrett himself had haunted her. She still couldn't imagine what had come over her on New Year's Eve to let herself be kissed by the man. To kiss him in return. She'd just been so surprised when he did it. One minute, he'd been telling her how doomed Kelly and Mac were, and the next, he'd been kissing her as if she were the answer to every prayer he'd sent skyward.

And what a kiss. Kiss*es,* she corrected herself. Plural. There had been nearly a half dozen of them. She knew that, because, as insensate as she'd been at the time, she'd counted each and every one of them. And even if they had been chaste and soft and undemanding—well, sort of chaste, sort of soft but in no way undemanding—the touch of Garrett's mouth on hers had shaken Renee right down to the furthest reaches of her soul. In those few times their lips had touched, she'd experienced a shudder of arousal unlike anything she'd ever known.

Fireworks. Mystery. Magic. All of those things had been present in that one embrace. And all she'd been able to do was open her hand over his chest in a silent request for more.

But just as Garrett had lowered his head to hers to give her more, something had halted Renee—she still wasn't sure what. A sense of self-preservation, perhaps. Some vague, ill-defined knowledge that if she kissed him again, there would be no turning back. It made no sense for her to have such a reaction to a veritable stranger, but there it was nonetheless. Something in Garrett had spoken to something in her. Something dark, something raw, something needy. Something she knew she'd be much better off *not* exploring.

Not with a man who hadn't even bothered to call her to see where those few little kisses might lead. And certainly not with a man who'd said flat out that he thought marriage was a complete waste of time and a total farce.

Unfortunately, as unwilling as Renee was to explore the feelings he'd roused in her, she still hadn't been able to forget

about them. Or about Garrett. He'd crept into her thoughts
when she least expected and had wandered into her dreams at
night. And worse, when he did so, he had the very troubling
tendency to be at least partially naked.

And although three months had passed since their brief in-
terlude, she could still feel the soft brush of his mouth over
hers, could still taste the faint flavor of champagne on his lips,
could still inhale the dusky male scent of him that had surrounded her. Those three months might as well have been
three minutes, so vivid was her memory of that night.

And it was that memory, she was sure, that kept making
her question the wisdom of her impending—*upcoming*—wedding. Because less than an evening in Garrett's presence su-
perseded months in Lyle's. When Renee thought about happily
ever afters these days, Lyle was nowhere to be found. Instead,
a whiskey-eyed man with pale brown hair—a man who had
absolutely no interest in marriage—was the one who appeared
in Renee's plans for a future.

And that simply would not do.

She told herself she was totally distorting her memory of
Garrett Fortune, that *no one* could possibly be as wonderful
as she was remembering him. He was little more than a
stranger. The two of them had spoken for less than an hour.
The kisses they had shared had been no more than a celebratory welcome to the New Year.

It had *not* been the earth-shattering, mind-scrambling, li-
bido-twisting experience she kept recalling. It hadn't. And that
single incident certainly wasn't something that should influence her decision to marry Lyle.

She reminded herself again that she and her fiancé—she
ignored the roll of nausea that swept through her as the word
formed in her head—were a good…well, a good
enough…match. By mutual agreement—at least, Renee was
pretty sure the agreement had been mutual… She'd certainly
been all for it herself—they'd agreed to wait until their wedding night to make love. But even though there were no
fireworks in their relationship—yet, she told herself—even

though there was no mystery, no magic—yet—Renee could live her life quite...quite adequately with Lyle. She didn't need romance. She didn't need love. She didn't.

She didn't.

Although she liked to think she was a woman of the nineties, a woman who made up her own mind and planned her own destiny, she was old-fashioned enough to believe in fulfilling obligations, too. And she did have an obligation to her father, one that was none too small.

He'd put so much of his life on hold so she would be happy. He'd never remarried, because he'd worried that such a relationship might somehow leave Renee feeling edged out of his life. He'd forgone vacations because she'd been in school and unable to accompany him. He'd worked long hours to build a business that would insure a future for her. He'd spent a considerable amount of money on private schools, tutors, riding lessons, piano lessons, etiquette lessons. He'd made certain Renee had the best of everything.

Everything Reginald Riley had done since her birth had been with his daughter's welfare first and foremost in his mind. Renee couldn't possibly betray him now, couldn't possibly risk his losing everything he'd spent decades working to build. There was no way she could do that to him.

Or to herself, she reminded herself ruthlessly. It wasn't just her father's welfare at stake. Renee, too, stood to lose a lifetime of memories and mementos, of sentiment and souvenirs. Not to mention sacrificing the only way of life she'd ever known. Certainly she could get by without money and a social position. But she really would hate to see it all go.

In frustration, she raked a hand through her tangle of curls, wincing when she snagged one in the gaudy engagement ring Lyle had given her. Carefully, she freed her hair and gazed at the dazzling, exquisite, four-carat diamond marquise.

Never big on jewelry unless it was of the antique variety, Renee had picked out a simple, half-carat solitaire perched in a silver setting embellished with marcasite. But Lyle had laughed good-naturedly at her choice, assuring her there was no reason for her to "settle" for something so small and un-assuming, not when she was about to marry Lyle Norton. So he had bought this ring for her instead. The gem was brilliant. Beautiful. Breathtaking.

And Renee felt guilty as sin wearing it.

It just wasn't right, she told herself. Not the ring, not the dress, not her feelings, not Lyle. She sighed heavily as the doubts threatened to overcome her again, closed her eyes at the waves of uncertainty that tried to shatter her fragile conviction that marrying Lyle was the Right Thing to do. And as always happened when she felt such a tremor in her convictions, Renee knew there was just one thing for her to do.

Get a facial.

Oh, what the heck, and a manicure, too, since she'd been so good about kicking the nail-biting habit. A facial and manicure were always good antidotes to anxiety and indecision. A trip to the spa was just about the only way she knew to relax, if even for a short time.

Carefully, she hung the wedding dress on its hanger and zipped it into the nylon bag to protect it. After a quick check in the mirror of her lavender velvet tunic and leggings, she made her way to her car.

The spa was surprisingly busy for a Monday afternoon. Although she got in for her manicure right away, thanks to a last-minute cancellation, without an appointment for her facial, Renee was directed to the waiting room for what she knew could be a rather lengthy wait. She knew that because she'd shown up without an appointment lots of times over the past three months.

Unperturbed, however—hey, where else did she have to be?—she settled back in her chair, gazing at the pale pastels and silk flowers that adorned the room, tuning her ear to the muted strains of a delicate Bach piano concerto. And she tried to find some peace of mind in the soft beauty that surrounded her. But when even the soothing environment of the spa's waiting room couldn't calm her, she closed her eyes and tried to think of something—anything—besides her impend—uh, upcoming wedding.

Unfortunately, as usually happened, the moment she cleared her mind, Garrett entered it. Oh, well. At least, this time, he wasn't naked. Well, not *too* naked. She remembered him the way he'd been on New Year's Eve—with just a few more buttons unbuttoned than had actually been unbuttoned at the time—heard his low, masculine laughter, felt the brush of his warm, rough skin against her own, recalled the heat and scent of him as he lowered his head to hers again and again and—

"Renee? Renee Riley? Is that you?"

Her eyes snapped open at the summons, and the heated images of Garrett dissolved in a fine, fleeting fog. Immediately, though, another member of the fabulous Fortune family replaced him—Kate Fortune, the matriarch in charge of the whole shebang, Fortune Cosmetics as well as the Fortune clan.

"Hi, Mrs. Fortune," Renee said with a heartfelt smile, genuinely happy to see the other woman.

She liked Kate immensely, having met her on a number of occasions, usually when she was with Kelly, who worked as Kate's social secretary. Well, who *used* to work as Kate's social secretary, at least. These days, of course, Kelly had her hands full with almost-two-month-old Annie—not to mention Mac. But that was another story.

"Oh, please," Kate said with a smile as she folded herself into the chair beside Renee's, "how many times do I have to tell you—call me Kate."

Renee smiled. "Yes, ma'am."

Kate shook her head ruefully, but smiled. "So how are you, dear? Kelly tells me you're getting married this month."

Another roll of nausea swept through Renee's belly. Striving for an enthusiasm she was nowhere close to feeling, forcing a smile that felt anything but happy, she said, "Um, yeah, as a matter of fact, I am, uh…getting married. This month. Yepper. Getting married. That's me."

Kate's eyebrows shot up in surprise. "Well, my goodness,

don't be so overjoyed. That smile is about to blind me, and
you're making a spectacle of yourself with that dance of joy.''

Renee did manage a chuckle at that. "I'm sorry," she said.
"It's just…"

"What?"

She shook her head. "Nothing. Never mind."

Kate eyed her thoughtfully. "Kelly seems to be of the opinion that the man you're planning to marry isn't quite…oh,
shall we say…Mr. Right.''

"Well, who's to say what constitutes Mr. Right. Right?"
She forced another chuckle that she hoped sounded carefree
and gave a toss of her head that had always gone a long way
toward convincing people she was completely consumed by
joie de vivre. Whatever that was.

But Kate Fortune was much too perceptive to buy the act.
Renee had long ago gotten the feeling that Kate saw way more
than people wanted her to see. And there was a keenness to
the way she was eyeing Renee that was more than a little
unsettling. As if she were making plans—big plans—for her
immediate future.

"Kelly was right," Kate said softly. "You're about to make
a terrible mistake, aren't you, dear?"

Renee gaped at her. Certainly Kelly had often enough crit-
icized her decision to marry Lyle, telling Renee she should
wait for the real thing—true love—regardless of her obligation
to her father. As if Kelly had any right to make judgments on
that score, seeing as how she'd married for reasons only mar-
ginally better than Renee's. In spite of the reasons for it,
though, Kelly's marriage was turning out to be a better arrangement than anyone had thought it would be. She and Mac
had come to truly care for each other.

It was something that had served to hearten Renee over the
last few months, allowed her to tell herself that she and Lyle
could make a go of it in the long run. Maybe, in time, the two
of them really would have feelings of affection for each other,
as Kelly and Mac did. Maybe. In time. She supposed it was
possible.

But then, theoretically speaking, it was also possible that the earth might go spinning out of its orbit any minute now and crash into the sun.

So all Renee could manage in response to Kate's admonition was a softly uttered, "Excuse me?"

"Kelly's worried about you, dear," Kate said. "As any good friend would be. She's afraid you're making a colossal error in not marrying for love, one you'll live to regret."

Before Renee had a chance to object, Kate, evidently having read her thoughts, hurried on. "Yes, I know, Kelly was in much the same boat, having married for reasons other than love herself. Which is why she knows what's in store for you if you make the wrong decision. Why don't you tell me all about it?"

Renee knew that was the last thing she could do. Kate was a nice woman, and she seemed to genuinely care about what Renee was going through, but this wasn't a conversation to have with someone who wasn't a close friend or family member. Kate was a local icon and a massively successful businesswoman, the last kind of person Renee would think of turning to when it came to girl talk.

In spite of that, however, she heard herself say, "Mrs. Fortune, what do you think is more important? Family obligation or true love?"

Kate offered her a knowing smile. "Well, certainly it's no secret how important I think family is. But that true love business, well… There's a reason poets and troubadours have stayed in business for thousands of years."

Renee thought about that, then said, "But lawyers and accountants have stayed in business for a long time, too, working out the details of marriages that take place for economic and social reasons."

"True," Kate conceded. "But they don't have as much of that kind of work as they used to."

"Neither do the poets and troubadours," Renee pointed out.

Kate didn't disagree. What she did say was, "You don't love the man you're going to marry, do you?"

"No," Renee replied without hesitation, knowing there was no point in denying that. "I don't love him. But he's a good man, and the arrangement will benefit my family."

Kate nodded. "And you think that's very important."

"Yes. I do. And in time, it's possible that I could come to love him." Unfortunately, Renee didn't utter the words with quite the conviction she had hoped to. She didn't quite *feel* the conviction she had hoped to, either.

"Is your obligation to your family more important than your own happiness?" Kate asked.

That, unfortunately, Renee couldn't answer. Because deep down, she did not *know* the answer. So she remained silent.

Kate watched her closely for a long time, then reached for her handbag. As she opened it and searched through its contents, she told Renee, "I think you have a lot of thinking to do, and I think you need some time—and some distance—that would allow you to do it."

Renee shook her head. "I don't have any time. The wedding is only a week away."

Without looking up, Kate told her, "All kinds of things can happen in a week, Renee. *All* kinds of things."

"I don't know, Mrs. Fortune, I—"

"Aha," Kate said, cutting her off. "Here they are." With a dramatic jangle, she withdrew a ring of keys and searched it quickly before deftly removing one. Then, with what Renee could only call a twinkle in her eye, she extended it.

"What's that?" she asked.

"The key to happiness," Kate said cryptically.

Renee smiled nervously. "I don't understand."

"You need some time to think," the other woman reiterated, "and you need a quiet place to do it. I just happen to have such a place at my disposal. I've used it myself on a number of occasions when I've needed to get away to gather my thoughts and make big decisions. And I frequently loan it to friends who find themselves in a similar position."

"And where would this place be?" Renee asked warily.

Kate smiled. "Wyoming."

"Wyoming?" Renee echoed incredulously. "I can't go to Wyoming. I'm getting married in a week."

Kate arched one elegant brow inquisitively. "Are you, dear?"

Renee swallowed hard and somehow forced herself to nod.

"Then consider this my wedding present to you," Kate said. "Some time away before the big event, to rest and relax and prepare yourself for the lifelong journey that awaits you upon your return."

Oh, God, Renee thought. She didn't like the sound of that at all. *A lifelong journey.*

"Mrs. Fortune, I appreciate the offer, but—"

"But what, dear?"

Renee sighed fitfully. "I can't go. I have too many things to do here."

"Such as?"

"Well, there's...um..."

Actually, even though the wedding was only a week away, there really wasn't that much for her to do. Lyle had insisted on a small wedding, because a large one would be too time-consuming and his work hours would prohibit him from participating. Renee hadn't disagreed. Their guest list barely numbered two dozen. They were planning to marry at his mother's house, and Mrs. Norton was taking care of all the arrangements. The caterer, musicians, photographer, florist, everyone was lined up and ready to go. All that was left was for everyone to show up on time, Renee included.

Now why had she thought that? she wondered. Of course she would be showing up on time. All Mrs. Fortune was saying was that she should get away from the stress of wedding planning for a little while, to relax and enjoy her final days as a single woman. And why did the phrase "final days" have such a fatal ring to it, as if she'd been bound over for execution?

Renee knew she could use a small rest—even a short one. She did feel more exhausted lately than she should, and entering a marriage fatigued wasn't a good idea. And what better way to rest than by traveling to a place where she didn't know anyone, where no one knew her, where she would have no obligations, no responsibilities, no requirements save taking it easy?

She didn't have to stay long, she told herself. Only a few days, long enough to reassure herself that she was making the right decision. Because marrying Lyle, she was sure, was indeed the right decision.

The timing of Kate's offer was actually very good. Lyle was out of town again—on business, naturally—and wouldn't be returning until the day before the wedding. The rest would do Renee good. She hadn't been sleeping well at all, thanks to all those dreams about Garrett.

Without realizing she had agreed to take Kate up on the offer, Renee found herself reaching slowly for the key the woman held out to her. But before she could grasp it, Kate released it, and the key fell easily right into the palm of Renee's hand.

"You'll be going to the Final Destination Ranch in Last Resort, Wyoming," Kate said with a smile.

Gee, could there possibly be anything more symbolic than that? Renee wondered.

"There's a little guest cabin on the property that's removed from the main house," Kate continued. "It's private and quiet, and perfect for your needs. I'll call the manager this afternoon and tell him to expect you this evening."

"This evening?" Renee echoed. "Oh, I couldn't possibly leave today. I have to go home and pack, tell my father and Lyle where I'm going and—"

"I'll tell your father," Kate volunteered. "It's been ages since I spoke to him, and this will give me the perfect excuse to call. Then he can tell your fiancé."

Renee opened her mouth to object, but Kate hurried on before she had a chance.

"And you need pack only the barest essentials. Everything you could ever need or want in life is on that ranch. Trust me."

"But I have to make travel arrangements and—"

"You can take the Fortune jet," Kate interrupted breezily, as if she were offering the use of a bicycle and nothing more. She rose from her chair, evidently forgetting that she had come to the spa for some reason other than taking charge of Renee's life. "I'll call and take care of all the arrangements for you. Just be at the Fortune hangar at the airport in two hours—I'll write down the directions for you—and you can be at the ranch in time for dinner."

She withdrew a pad and pen from her handbag, quickly jotted some instructions, then tore the slip of paper off and handed to Renee. "And, Renee," she added with a sweet smile, "do enjoy yourself, dear."

Three

———

"**R**eggie? Kate Fortune calling. It's been ages since we spoke—how *are* you?"

"Kate! It *has* been a long time. How nice to hear from you. I'm doing well. You?"

"Couldn't be better. Listen, I have to talk to you about Renee."

"What about Renee?"

"I ran into her this morning, and we had a very interesting conversation."

"Did she tell you she's getting married this month? To Lyle Norton, no less?"

"Oh, I can just hear the pride and joy in your voice when you say that, Reggie. Yes, we did discuss the fact that she's getting married soon."

"I couldn't be happier about the arrangement."

"Oh, I'll just bet you couldn't. That Lyle Norton is some-thing, all right. But listen, here's the thing. Renee looked *aw-*

fully tired to me so I offered her a place to retreat to for a few days, so she could get a little rest.''

''Retreat to? What do you mean, 'retreat to?'''

''Just that. A small retreat I have at my disposal, a place where I go for a little while when I need to rest or sort things out.''

''Sort things out?''

''You know…make big decisions, think about the repercussions of my actions, that kind of thing.''

''Think about the reper—''

''And I gave the key to Renee and told her to take a few days off from the wedding plans, so that *she* could get some rest and clear *her* head.''

''Clear her—''

''She won't be gone long. But circumstances being what they were, she had to leave in a hurry.''

''And just what were the circum—''

''So I told her I'd call you and let you know where she is so you wouldn't be worried.''

''And just where is she?''

''Wyoming.''

''Wyoming?''

''If you need her, call me, and I'll get in touch with her and tell her to contact you. And don't worry about her—she's by no means alone where she is. If she needs anything—anything at all—there's someone there to take care of her.''

''Kate, what are you up to?''

''Up to? Me? Why, nothing. But just between you and me, Reggie, I think if Faye were alive to see what you've done, she'd be appalled.''

''What *I've* done? What are you talking about?''

''Arranging a marriage for your daughter this way. It's archaic. Faye would have a fit if she were here to see it. She was always *such* a romantic dear. You were, too, once upon a time. You should be ashamed of yourself now, for making Renee feel as if she has an obligation to marry a man she doesn't love simply to save a business you've managed badly."

"Kate, this is none of your—"

"Renee will be fine. You needn't worry. Not about her welfare, at any rate. She's perfectly safe. She'll be home in a few days. You have my word. But right now, I think she needs some time to herself. Alone. Well, pretty much alone, anyway."

"What she needs is—"

"I'll call her and let her know I spoke to you. Ta ta, Reggie. Do have a nice day."

With a purr of delight, Kate Fortune dropped the telephone receiver into its cradle, folded her arms over the top of her desk and sighed contentedly. There. Let Reggie Riley stew over *that* for a few days. See how *he* liked having control taken out of *his* hands for a change.

Honestly. Sending your own daughter on a guilt trip and making her feel obligated to marry a man to whom she was completely unsuited—not to mention a man she didn't love and who didn't love her in return—just so you could save your floundering company. Reggie really should be ashamed of himself. Faye Riley must be spinning in her grave over this one. There was no way Kate could turn her back on something as wrong as all this.

Renee Riley was a sweet, kind child who deserved better. And if Kate had any say in the matter, better was exactly what she was going to get. Thank goodness Kelly had seen fit to tell Kate what was going on.

She glanced at her watch and grinned with *much* satisfaction. Right about now, Garrett would be outside the main house on the Final Destination, taking care of the numerous afternoon chores that never seemed to end. There was no way he'd be able to hear his telephone ringing. So Kate picked up the phone again and began to punch the first of eleven long-distance numbers that would contact him.

And when his answering machine picked up at the other end, she said, "Oh, Garrett, dear, you *know* how much I *hate* to talk to your machine. Ah, well, there's nothing else for it, I suppose. I'm sorry for calling at the last minute this way, but I've been absolutely swamped with work. I just wanted to tell you that I'm sending a friend of mine your way who'll be staying at the cabin for a few days. I do hope you'll make her feel welcome. She has some *extremely* serious life choices to work out....''

"Aunt Kate, I swear to God, I'll get you for this."

Garrett Fortune uttered the words aloud—even though there was no one around for miles to hear them—and glared at the answering machine on his desk as if *it* were to blame for the message he'd just played from his great-aunt. The last thing he wanted or needed was the arrival of some flaky grande dame of Minneapolis society. There was no way he had time to play houseboy to one of Kate's high-society friends.

He didn't care if she *did* own the damned cabin. The ranch was his. He'd received the deed just last week.

Of course, there was nothing he could do about it now, seeing as how the woman would be arriving in...oh, about fifteen minutes.

Extremely difficult life choices, he repeated to himself, disgusted. Yeah, right. The only kind of life choice his great aunt's friends probably ever had to make was whether to serve bouillabaisse or bisque for an appetizer.

He could picture his guest already, some high-society matron with overly coiffed hair and overly manicured nails, trailing a half dozen oversize suitcases and at least that many of those irritating undersize dogs in her wake. She'd be suffering from some major trauma—her daughter was marrying a gas pump jockey, for example, or her son had decided to study hairdressing instead of medicine—and she'd be beside herself with self-pity because her life was going to hell in a handbasket. Then she'd start calling Garrett at the main house day and night, as if he were Julie-your-cruise-director and room service at the Ritz-Carlton all rolled into one.

Damn. This was to have been the week Garrett started turning what had always been Kate's weekend getaway into a working ranch. For too long the Final Destination's potential had been completely wasted. Hundreds of acres of prime grazing land had provided little more than a beautiful backdrop for a house that had served as a vacation home for the Fortune family and sundry friends.

When Kate had set Garrett up to manage the place a little over a year ago, he'd looked forward to finally having the chance to install all the improvements necessary to make it the working ranch he'd envisioned since he was a kid. But wanting to have a real stake in the operation, Garrett had offered to buy the place from her instead. Kate had agreed to go along with the deal, provided she kept the guest cabin and surrounding property.

And now Garrett was about to see a childhood dream come true. He would make the Final Destination a ranch that could turn a tidy little profit year after year. Eventually, he planned to retire from what was already just part-time legal consulting to run the place full-time. He was itching to get started on his improvements. The last thing he needed this week was a houseguest ruining what little free time he'd planned to give himself.

"Dammit," he muttered to no one in particular. Then, just for good measure, he kicked the desk.

At least the woman would be staying at the cabin, he thought, which would put a good half mile between them. Maybe he had enough time to rig the telephone so she wouldn't be able to call the main house during her stay.

The crunch of gravel in the driveway made Garrett's plan evaporate, and he prepared himself to be overrun by expensive luggage, killer lapdogs and a woman more suited to the Four Seasons Hotel than a Wyoming ranch. But when he opened the front door, what greeted him bore no resemblance to any of his ideas. Because there, against the backdrop of a wide-open sky stained pink and purple and orange in the wake of a setting sun, was a blast from his past he wasn't likely to forget.

Renee Riley.

Oh, man...

She was standing on the opposite side of a bland, four-door sedan that just screamed rental, reaching into the back seat for something—so she wasn't paying attention to him. Which was good, because it meant she couldn't see him gazing at her with what he hated to think was probably a profound, poetic longing.

Damn.

With the spectacular sunset looming behind her and with those riotous curls falling forward, obscuring part of her face, she almost looked like a painting. One of those Pre-Raphaelites he recalled from a humanities prerequisite at college—a lush, rounded woman gathering wheat at dusk. Garrett shook his head to clear it of the odd idea and tried—without much success—to tamp down the heat and desire that jumped to the fore. This was all he needed—Renee Riley as a houseguest.

Kate's houseguest, he reminded himself. So *she* was the one who had some serious life choices to work out.

What kind of life choices could a woman that young have to ponder that she would exile herself to the very back of beyond? Because that's exactly what the Final Destination was. A retreat in the fullest sense of the word, tucked in the middle of nowhere, barely in reach of society. They were on the very edge of available electricity and water, too far out for any kind of decent TV or radio reception. This was a place to do two things—raise cattle and get away from life.

It suited Garrett perfectly.

Renee, however... Well, she didn't quite seem the exile type. On the contrary, the impression he'd received of her at Mac's wedding was of a warm, outgoing woman who doubtless made friends faster than most people made messes, someone who thrived in social surroundings.

Even though they'd only spent a short time together, they'd shared a surprisingly meaningful conversation. Among other things. And somehow, in that brief time, Renee had crawled under Garrett's skin and set up housekeeping there. Over the last three months, no matter how hard he'd tried—and he'd tried awfully damned hard—he hadn't been able to drive her out of his system. She lingered constantly at the fringes of his thoughts, crept into his brain at the oddest moments and just more or less left him tied in knots.

All because of a few little kisses that had left him thinking, *What if…*

Which was another thing he wished he could figure the hell out. He'd shared more than a couple of chaste kisses with more than a couple of women, but no encounter he'd ever had with the opposite sex had come close to shaking him up the way a few little pecks with Renee had. There had been nothing to that embrace, he tried to tell himself, not for the first time. Nothing. But it had haunted him like no other experience he'd ever shared with a woman.

It made no sense. She was too young, too naive, too insignificant to have this effect on him. But as she straightened and hauled an oversize tote bag over her shoulder, slinging her hair back in the process, the evening breeze nudged a dark curl over her forehead. And Garrett, God help him, found himself wanting to run to the yard to tuck the errant strand of hair where it belonged.

He just wanted to touch her. Badly. As he'd wanted to touch her for three months. Three long, agonizing months. And now here she was, almost within reach, as if someone were bestowing upon him a wondrous gift. Someplace deep down inside Garrett, a little spark he would have sworn had been doused years ago flickered to life, sputtered a bit, then kindled into a small, fragile flame. And strangely enough, he felt a smile—an honest-to-God genuinely happy smile—curl his lips for the first time in years.

When she lifted her fingers to push her hair out of her eyes, the dying sunlight exploded in a flash of blue and copper through something big and bright on her finger. Her ring finger. Of her *left* hand. Garrett's smile fell instantly, and deep down inside him, the flame that had begun to grow warmer was gutted completely. Something in his belly clenched tight as a fist.

An engagement ring. Somehow, even though the space of a front yard separated them, he knew that was what had caused the brief slash of light. And he realized at once what her *serious life choices* must be about.

Looked like Renee Riley had bagged herself a rich husband. Or, at least, she was about to. Well, well, well.

Suddenly that odd conversation they'd had New Year's Eve wasn't quite so odd anymore. Evidently Renee hadn't just been talking about her friend Kelly when she'd said marriage needn't be based on love. Apparently, Renee, too, was motivated by something other than hearts and flowers when it came to tying herself to another human being. And judging by the size of that rock on her finger, Garrett was pretty sure he knew what that something was.

Cold, hard cash.

When she straightened and made her way to the other side of the car, he saw that she was carrying a small weekender to match the tote slung over her shoulder. Her attire was the epitome of uptown girl on vacation, an ensemble in a soft, velvety fabric that draped over her lush curves with *much* affection, its color rivaling the deep lavenders that stained the sky behind her. He let his gaze travel hungrily over her from head to toe, narrowing his eyes when he noted her feet.

Because on those feet were what appeared to be two blocks of wood with leather hammered onto them to keep them in place. Shoes that were in no way suitable to the wet, marshy ground between her and the front door, which was where she was headed, in spite of the fact that the walkway led to the back door. Sure enough, the moment she stepped off the gravel drive and into the yard, the grass sucked that shoe right off her foot.

"Ooh," she muttered in exasperation as her stocking-clad foot went onto the ground with an annoying *thwuck*.

The unsteady landing threw off her balance, and for a moment, he thought she was going to pitch face first into the yard. Instinctively, he descended the front steps, but she righted herself quickly, capably—except for the fact that her stocking got soaked with muddy water—by the time he reached the bottom stair.

Growling something unintelligible under her breath, she shoved her foot carelessly into her shoe and moved forward again. This time, she took greater care to watch where she was going, focusing her gaze on the stubby yellow grass, testing the ground experimentally before placing her foot down firmly. So intent was she on her progress, in fact, that she didn't even seem to notice Garrett standing on the bottom stair of the front steps.

Not until she stood in front of him. When she drew near enough to sense his presence, though, she finally glanced up, wearing that dazzling smile that he recalled way too well from New Year's Eve. And just as it had that night, it fell the moment she realized whom she'd run into.

"What are *you* doing here?" she blurted by way of a greeting.

Stung by the fact that she appeared to be in no way happy to see him—and angry at himself for even *being* stung by such a thing—he replied gruffly, "Well, that's a hell of a way to say hello to your host."

She arched her eyebrows in surprise. "My host? I thought Kate owned the Final Destination."

Garrett shook his head. "Not since I bought it from her. Now all Aunt Kate owns is the guest cabin and the acre of land surrounding it. The rest of the property is mine."

Renee blinked a few times, as if the effort might make what he'd just said a little clearer. "Oh. Then I guess that means you're the manager?" she asked.

He nodded. "Yep."

She narrowed her eyes at him, studying him at length, and it bugged Garrett to kingdom come and back that she obviously didn't feel the electricity whipping around them like a tropical storm. Especially since the sizzle of heat burning up the air between them was as plain to him as a cattle prod to the kneecap would be.

Finally, she said, "But I thought you worked as a legal consultant for the Fortune Corporation."

"I do work as a legal consultant for the Fortune Corporation," he told her. "Part-time. From here."

"Oh."

"And just how did you know that I work as a legal consultant for the Fortune Corporation?"

Two bright spots of pink stained her cheeks, and he felt some small satisfaction that he'd finally gotten an emotional reaction out of her. Okay, so maybe embarrassment wasn't exactly the emotion he'd been hoping for. It was a start.

"I, uh…" She swallowed with difficulty before continuing. "I might have, um, oh, asked Kelly a question or two about you over the last few months."

This time Garrett was the one to narrow his eyes. "And why would you be asking Kelly about me?"

Again, color suffused her face, though this time he sensed the reason for it was less embarrassment and more…guilt? "No reason," she said quickly.

"Well, what did Kelly tell you about me?" he asked, wondering why he cared. "Aside from my job credentials, I mean."

"Nothing," she squeaked. Actually squeaked. Now, if that wasn't incriminating, he didn't know what was.

"Really?" he asked.

She nodded, a vigorous, conspicuous gesture that was in no way convincing. "Really," she assured him. "Just that you work as a legal consultant for Fortune and that you're divor—" She slapped a hand viciously over her mouth, as if she needed to shut herself up immediately and that was the best way she had at her disposal.

"That I'm divorced," he finished for her.

Garrett's back went up when he realized there had been some gossiping going on about him within the Fortune ranks. Not that he was surprised—news generally spread like wildfire in his family. If one Fortune sneezed, before a half hour was up, the rest of them had replied, "Bless you." And not that Garrett cared that he was being gossiped about. Well, not much, anyway. Hell, the family had been talking about him for years now.

But for the first time, he found himself wishing he knew what his relatives were saying about him. Because for the first time, Renee Riley was the one receiving the information. Though why that should make a difference, he couldn't possibly have said.

So he pushed away his concerns and demanded flat out, "Did the newest Mrs. Fortune also fill you in on all the gory details of my marriage and divorce? That must have put you off your lunch, but good."

Renee shook her head and kept her hand planted firmly in place, revealing nothing of what her friend might have told her about Garrett. Still, he could pretty well imagine what Kelly had said. Probably the same thing the rest of the Fortune family said about him. That he was ill-tempered and bad-mannered. That he was humorless and joyless. That he'd been that way for years—ever since his wife tried to drain his bank account before throwing him over for another man—and that nothing was likely to change him back to his old, fun-loving, happy-go-lucky self.

Not that he *ever* wanted to revert to that annoying, idealistic, gullible sap. On the contrary, he worked hard to live down to everyone's expectations.

When he realized Renee was studying him with more interest than he cared to acknowledge, he stepped down and turned his attention to stubbing the toe of his boot into the wet grass. His blue jeans and denim shirt were filthy, he noted, from working outside most of the day. For some reason, that bothered him—being dirty around Renee Riley. She was just too damned *clean* for his comfort. In more ways than one.

Without looking up, he said, "So what are *you* doing here?"

She dropped her hand from her mouth, and Garrett watched

it fall to her side, honing his gaze on the elegantly manicured fourth finger, where a diamond the size of the Tetons winked at him. Just how much money did her husband-to-be have, he wondered, to be able to afford a rock like that? Must be some old geezer who'd spent his entire life hoarding his wealth.

"Oh," she said, stirring him from his none-too-charitable speculation. "That. Well. You see. Um. It's like this." She sighed deeply, as if that might rev up her vocabulary some, then tried again. "Mrs. Fortune—your aunt Kate, I mean— told me it would be okay if I spent a few days at her cabin."

Garrett nodded. "Why?"

"Why?" The question seemed to totally stump her.

"Yeah. Why?"

"Well. It's because I, uh… See, I'm—that is, I…"

"You're getting married."

Her eyes widened in surprise. "Mrs. Fortune told you about that?"

"No. That big hunk of ice you're wearing on your left hand just sorta put the idea into my head. Go figure."

And just why did he sound like a jealous lover all of a sudden? he wondered. It was none of his business what Renee Riley did, matrimonywise or otherwise. If she wanted to spend the rest of her life marrying old geezers and collecting one mountain-size diamond after another, it was no affair of his.

Affair. Now why did *that* word suddenly make his heart beat faster than a heart had a right to beat? And why was he having such mean thoughts about a woman who, until a few minutes ago, he'd been recalling as sweet and naive? He had to get a hold of himself.

When he looked up, he saw that her attention, too, had fallen to the engagement ring. She wiggled her fingers as if trying to get maximum sparkle for the gesture, but instead of looking predatory, she looked…well, she looked kind of sad.

"I guess it is a dead giveaway, isn't it?" she said softly. "It's not the ring I wanted, but…"

Garrett finished her sentence for her, keeping the observation to himself. It wasn't the ring she wanted, but she'd settle for whatever she could get, he guessed.

He shook his head viciously, trying to rid it of all the crazy notions ricocheting through it. He had to get away from Renee Riley. Otherwise he was going to turn into a stark, raving jerk and say something even *he* would be hard-pressed to forgive.

"The cabin is a good piece from the main house," he said, jutting a thumb over his shoulder in the general direction of Kate's dwelling. "Do you have any other shoes you could wear to walk over? Those aren't exactly appropriate for the landscape."

"I didn't have time to change," she told him.

Suddenly she seemed very, very tired. Something inside Garrett turned over at the fatigue in her voice, and he found himself wanting to pick her up and carry her off to bed. Not necessarily to *her* bed, though. And certainly not for the sleep she so obviously needed.

"It's all right," she continued, scattering his strange thoughts. "These will be okay, now that I know what I'm up against. Just point me in the right direction."

Like hell he'd point her in the right direction, Garrett thought. While they'd been standing there jawing, it had become almost fully dark. By the time they reached the cabin, it would be black as pitch. She could walk within feet of the place and miss it, then wind up coyote food before dawn.

"Give me your stuff," he instructed her.

At his command, her expression became as imperious as a queen's. Even so, he was glad to see she was feeling something other than that tired melancholy that had clouded her face moments ago.

"Excuse me?" she asked.

He rolled his eyes. "Give me your stuff, please," he corrected himself, "and I'll show you the way to Kate's cabin."

"Oh." She almost looked disappointed that he wasn't going to behave like a great, hulking ogre. "I guess that would be okay."

With reluctance, she surrendered her weekender bag, and

he slung it easily over his shoulder. Then he tilted his head in a silent suggestion that she should follow him and spun to head in that direction.

But as the shadowy outline of Kate's cabin came into sight, he decided that a good half mile was in no way enough distance to put between himself and Renee Riley.

Four

Renee watched the broad back of the man walking in front of her and tried—again—with no success—again—to make her heart stop pounding so ferociously. She was beginning to feel dizzy with all the zinging in the strings of her heart.

She inhaled a deep breath and held it for a moment, and gradually her pulse rate began to steady. Of course, holding her breath like that only compounded her dizziness, and before she could stop herself, she stumbled over a rock that came out of nowhere to say howdy to her shoe. She pitched forward, instinctively splaying a hand on Garrett's back—Garrett's big, broad, muscular back—to right herself.

Ooh, big mistake, she realized immediately. Because in addition to giving her more knowledge of his physical well-being than was healthy for a confused and aroused—not to mention engaged—woman to know, the action also caused him to spin around and face her. Evidently, he thought she was about to fall down, because he quickly curled strong fingers around her upper arm to pull her close.

"Are you okay?" he asked, clearly breathless.

She was surprised that a little walk like this would wind him so. Then again, she was having a little trouble breathing herself. But her ragged respiration had nothing to do with their stroll to Kate's cabin and everything to do with the heat that seeped through her sleeve where Garrett's fingers had landed.

"I'm okay," she lied, the words coming out a little strangled. "Totally...totally okay. Just a little, uh... I'm okay," she reiterated, unable to think of anything else to say. Well, anything that wouldn't get her into big, big trouble where Garrett Fortune and his hot fingers and broad back were concerned.

But he didn't seem quite convinced of her okayness, because he didn't let go of her arm. "Just watch your step," he said, and somehow, she got the feeling he wasn't talking about the rock she'd stumbled over. "Usually the path is clear, but there was some bad weather recently that really messed things up."

Renee pushed aside the notion that there was a double meaning to his warning. "I'm okay," she repeated. "It takes more than a little bad weather to mess me up. You can let go of me now."

Even in the darkness, she could see the look of surprise that crossed his face, as if he honestly hadn't realized he was still holding on to her. Immediately, he recoiled, as if she were an icky slug that was clinging to his finger, one that wouldn't be shaken off, no matter how hard he tried.

As they neared the cabin, Renee pulled her tote bag forward and fished the key out of the little pocket in front. But before she could place it in the lock, Garrett relieved her of it, then turned it—and the doorknob—himself. Before she could comment on his forwardness—she didn't care if he *was* her host, this was totally unnecessary and not a little unnerving, seeing as how she suddenly, for some really bizarre reason, wanted to slam the door behind them and lock it up tight so she could have him all to herself—he entered and began turning on lights.

Oh, boy, she really had to get hold of herself, she thought as she followed him inside. The last thing she needed was to be locked up with Garrett Fortune. Mainly because she had no idea what to do with a man like him.

Well, other than wrestle him to the ground and have her way with him. If she could just figure out what, precisely, was involved in having one's way with someone. Here she was, stranded in the wilds of Wyoming with a man like Garrett, and she didn't have the first idea what to do with him. Damn, this was a rotten time to be a virgin.

Stop it, she commanded herself. She was being ridiculous. She barely knew the man, even if they *had* both played key roles in a wedding that had united two of their loved ones. Even if they *had* shared an intimate little heart-to-heart on the pros and cons of marital responsibility. Even if they *had* exchanged a handful of kisses that had left her feeling lonely and lost, nostalgic and needy. Even if he *did* still haunt her dreams on an almost nightly—and certainly erotic—basis.

"I didn't know you were coming, so the place isn't ready for habitation," he said as he went about his task, rousing her from what had threatened to become an overwhelming preoccupation. "I just got the message from Aunt Kate off my answering machine a few minutes before you arrived. Otherwise, I could have at least aired the place out and turned on the heat."

Renee wrapped her arms snugly around her body. Despite the cool air, however, she felt immediately comfortable. Walls of honey-colored pine were hung with dozens of dried wreaths and hanging herbs that made the room pungent with a clean, spicy aroma. The furniture was rough-hewn, possibly hand crafted, upholstered in colors reminiscent of desert and forest alike. Scattered about the floor were area rugs woven of similarly earthy hues. Windows, completely lacking in drapery, wrapped three sides of the living room and probably provided a spectacular view during the day. At night, however, they would afford her absolutely no privacy. Not that there seemed to be anyone around for miles who might invade that privacy, she told herself.

Well, no one except Garrett.

She nudged the thought away and focused again on the cabin that would be her home for the next few days. Even without heat, the living room warmed her. However, that didn't stop Garrett from moving right to the fireplace to start laying out a fire.

"You don't have to do that," she told him. Though whether her urging came from the fact that she was fully capable of building her own fire or because she wanted him gone as quickly as possible, she couldn't quite say.

"The furnace unit is old and not exactly reliable," he explained without looking up from his efforts. "Even though it's small, it's going to take a while to get this place heated up. A fire will help. It's been getting awfully cold at night. Spring's slow to come to Wyoming sometimes."

"Still, I can—"

"It'll just take me a few minutes."

Renee inhaled a slow breath, counted calmly to ten and tried to will her heartbeat to its regular pace. Had she had any inkling Garrett lived at the Final Destination, Renee never would have set foot in the state of Wyoming.

He was part of the reason she needed to get away for a few days. In fact, he may well be her *biggest* reason—her biggest problem—because memories of him kept superseding thoughts of Lyle. Now, instead of escaping Garrett, she was going to have to deal with having him close at hand.

Close at hand. Not the best way to be thinking about him, she decided. Because at the moment, her hands seemed to want to get as close to Garrett as they could as soon as was feasibly possible. She was helpless to keep her attention off him as he laid the fire.

He was built like a freight truck, his shoulders wide enough to nearly eclipse the small hearth. The well-worn fabric of his denim work shirt strained against the taut, firm flesh of his back, and the dance of muscle and sinew every time he changed positions made her heart hammer wildly. His waist was narrow, his hips trim and his…his…well, his tushie was quite…quite…

Renee sighed wistfully, her fingers curling possessively into her palms. Why did Garrett's presence in a room affect her this way? she wondered. A simple conversation, one that had occurred three months ago, should not leave a person feeling so muzzy-headed and turned on.

She and Lyle had spent infinitely more time together, had engaged in considerably more conversation, and her fiancé was every bit as attractive as Garrett was. Well, almost every bit as attractive, she amended reluctantly. So why couldn't Lyle heat her blood this way, simply by…by moving? By breathing? By *being?*

Of all people, why did it have to be Garrett, who thought marriage was a farce and a waste of time? Then again, considering what Kelly had told Renee of Garrett's marriage, she supposed she could hardly blame him for his opinion. Still…

The scratch of a match caught her attention, and she watched as Garrett squatted in front of the fireplace to be certain the dry tinder caught and the flames spread higher. When he rose and turned toward her, his face was ruddy with the heat from the fire, and his gaze was focused entirely on her.

"That ought to get you through until bedtime," he said. "By then, the furnace should be doing its job."

And if it isn't, will you come back and warm my bed for me?

Renee squeezed her eyes shut tight as the uncharacteristic thought unfurled in her head. Why on earth would she think such a thing? She, who'd never even experienced what went into warming a bed, having never had her bed—or herself—warmed like that in the first place.

"Thanks," she managed to say. "I appreciate it."

When she forced her eyes open again, Garrett hadn't moved. He stood there looking at her, obviously lost in thought.

"What?" she asked, unable to curb her curiosity.

The one-word question seemed to stump him, because although he opened his mouth to respond, nothing came out.

"Garrett?" she said in an effort to encourage him.

It was the first time she'd said his name aloud in his presence, and the feel of it rolling off her tongue was much too intimate, much too sweet, much too easy for her comfort. The sound of it seemed to startle him, too, because his eyes widened, and he took a step closer.

Immediately, however, he checked himself. And he said, "I think we need to have a little talk about something."

"New Year's Eve," she blurted. "I know." Then, before he had a chance to comment, she rushed on. "Forget about it. Please. I know I have."

She could tell he didn't believe that any more than she did. "If you've forgotten about it, then how come that was the first thing that popped into your head when I told you we needed to talk about something?"

Gee, good question. She wished she had a good answer to go with it. "Well, uh…what else could we have to talk about?" she stammered. "That's the only time we've ever, um, spent any time together."

He nodded, but his jaw was clenched tight, as if he, too, were bothered by the recollection of that night. "Yeah, but for all you knew, I was just going to give you some information about the ranch that might make your stay here more enjoyable."

"Oh," she said flatly, embarrassment coiling in her stomach. "Is, uh, is that what you wanted to talk about?"

He shook his head. "No."

"Oh."

"I was going to talk about New Year's Eve."

"Oh."

"About those little kisses we shared."

"Oh."

"About how you shouldn't read any more into them than was there to begin with, because there was nothing to them."

Renee gaped at him. Now wait just a doggone minute.... "About how *I* shouldn't read any more into them?" she said. "What about *you?*"

Garrett gaped back, clearly surprised. "What about me?" he asked, his voice edged with warning.

Renee ignored it. "Sounds to me like maybe *you* read a lot more into those kisses than *I* did."

He settled his hands on his waist—that trim, sexy waist— and demanded, "And just what would give you that idea?"

She adopted a threatening pose of her own, tossing her tote bag onto the sofa before placing her hands on her hips. "Well, you're the one who brought it up."

"Yeah, but only because you've been standing there looking at me like I'm a big ol' piece of cherry pie you can't wait to devour."

She gaped again, even wider this time. "Like a big ol' piece of..." She expelled an incredulous sound as her voice trailed off, so profound was her disbelief—not that he would point out such a thing, mind you, but because he had caught her doing exactly what he'd accused her of doing.

In spite of her embarrassment at being discovered, however, she said, "In your dreams, pal. I like *my* desserts to be infinitely sweeter than you are."

Garrett frowned as he eyed Renee, feeling a deeper response than he was comfortable acknowledging. It was none of her damned business what his dreams had consisted of lately, even if she *had* played front and center in most of them—especially where her front and center were concerned. And just how many...desserts...had she sampled in the past, anyway?

"Look," she said, snapping him out of what had promised to be a really enjoyable bout of self-righteousness. "I've had a long day, and I don't want to argue with you, all right? I was fitted for a wedding dress that mocks me, I didn't get a facial that I really, really needed, I was accosted by your aunt Kate, I flew down here on a jet that was too small to even qualify for amoeba status, I have a dirty stocking stuck to my foot, and I ran into you. Now, if you don't mind, I'd like to call it a night and have a little time to myself, okay?''

Garrett hesitated before asking, ''How about breakfast tomorrow?''

She eyed him incredulously. ''After everything that's been said tonight, do you honestly think I'd like to have breakfast with you tomorrow?''

He shook his head, feigning a blandness he didn't feel. Renee's suggestion that they might share breakfast tomorrow morning—however negative—had him coming up with all kinds of ideas about how the two of them could spend the night before their morning meal. But all he said was, ''I wasn't asking you to have breakfast with *me*. I was asking what *you* plan to do about breakfast in the morning for yourself. And dinner tonight, for that matter, seeing as how there's no food in the cabin.''

Just like that, the steam she'd been building evaporated, and her shoulders slumped as if she suddenly carried the weight of the ages. ''Oh,'' she said in a very small voice. Then she roused herself some and added, ''Not to worry.'' she dipped her head toward the tote bag she'd tossed onto the sofa. ''I brought a few snacks with me. I'll make do.''

''Snacks aren't going to last long.''

She threw him a cryptic smile, then picked up the bag and began to unpack it with a triumphant flourish. ''Smoked salmon,'' she said proudly, holding a flat foil package aloft. She set it on the end table before reaching in to extract a can. ''Goose liver pâté,'' she continued before placing it next to the salmon. Then, ever victorious, she withdrew several other items as he watched, identifying each proudly as she went. ''Oysters. Artichoke hearts. Black olives. Caviar. Goldfish crackers. Dried apricots. And, it goes without saying,'' she concluded, withdrawing one final item, "a really big bag of Oreos."

"And to wash it down?" he asked wryly.

She smiled again, reached into the seemingly bottomless tote bag and withdrew a slender green bottle. "A nice fumé blanc," she told him. "Not too sweet, not too dry, with a citrusy bouquet to tease the olfactory senses and a playfulness that will dance on the palate. I have a nice Beaujolais, too, should I find myself in the mood for something a little more full-bodied. Satisfied?"

Garrett flattened his mouth into a thin line. "Raided your old man's pantry before coming, did you?"

She shook her head as she began to repack her feast. "No, I stopped by the supermarket. My father's not much of a gourmet. When it comes to snacking, he's definitely a saltine and peanut butter kind of guy."

"I wasn't talking about your father."

Confusion clouded her features. "Who else could you be talking about?"

"By 'old man,' I meant your fiancé," Garrett said, bothered by the unmistakable tint of jealousy that colored his words.

Her expression grew faintly puzzled. "For one thing, I'm not living with my fiancé. For another…" She hesitated before asking, "What makes you think he's old?"

Garrett shrugged, hoping the gesture looked more casual than it felt. "Just a figure of speech," he told her.

"It didn't sound like a figure of speech the way you used it. It sounded like you think my old man is, well, an old man."

He growled under his breath before reiterating, more emphatically this time, "It was a figure of speech."

She expelled a tired sound, as if she were too exhausted to continue with their conversation. "It was a figure of speech. Fine."

"Fine," he echoed.

"Good."

"Good."

"Just so we have that in the clear."

"We have that in the clear."

Nice to know *something* was in the clear, Garrett thought. Seeing as how whatever was going on between him and Renee was growing more and more muddled with every passing moment.

"Look, if you don't mind..." she said, her meaning obvious.

Garrett nodded. "Yeah, I'll shove off. Don't worry about me."

Not that she would, he knew. Renee Riley seemed to have a lot more on her mind than thoughts of him. And why that realization would irritate him so much was yet another reason to stay away from her.

Dammit, why couldn't he just forget about her? She was a woman who coveted the finer things in life, who snacked on the likes of smoked salmon, caviar and fumé blanc, who sat still long enough to have her already beautiful hands pampered and painted. She wore a ten-ton diamond and wished it were bigger. The picture he'd carried of her since New Year's Eve—of a nice, sweet, naive kid—had either been totally erroneous from the beginning, or else she had been turned by events that had occurred since that night.

Whoever Renee had been that night, she was another woman entirely now, a woman who valued wealth above all else in life. And there was no way in hell Garrett would *ever* get involved with another woman like that. Even if she did have eyes as green and bottomless as the ocean and a mouth red and ripe enough to make a man's blood boil over.

"There's a phone number tacked to the bulletin board by the phone in the kitchen," he said, gesturing that way. "If you need anything, call it. It'll ring at the main house."

She nodded, but said nothing. Somehow, Garrett got the feeling she *wanted* to say something, she just didn't follow through with it. So what could he do but bid her a quiet good-night and leave her alone, the way she clearly wanted him to leave her?

Renee Riley was everything he didn't need, everything he didn't want, everything he should avoid in a woman, he told himself as he closed the door of Kate's cabin and made his way to the main house. So why did he take his time walking home? Why were his instincts telling him to linger? Why was *avoiding* her at the very bottom of his list of things to do? But more than all those questions, one made its presence known far more insistently than others.

Just how long was Renee Riley planning to stay?

Five

When Renee awoke the following morning, it was to a symphony of wonderful sensations. A burst of sunshine tumbled through the bedroom window to warm her face, the cry of a felicitous mockingbird greeted her ear, and the clean aroma of dried rosemary drifted from the wreath hanging above her bed, filling her lungs with its fresh, clean fragrance. And all she could do was lie there with her eyes closed and her arms spread wide, silently thanking Kate Fortune for giving her this respite Renee would have sworn she didn't need.

She did need it. She needed to be away from home for a few days, needed a rest from the wedding plans. She really did have a lot of thinking to do. She knew that, because ever since laying eyes on Garrett Fortune last night, her brain—along with other body parts that were best left unidentified—had been abuzz with activity. And very little of it had been evidence of a sound mind or body.

Although she told herself she should do her thinking in a place far, far away from him—like maybe one of the nicer, more habitable moons of Jupiter—she might just be better off staying right where she was. The Final Destination was quiet, secluded, peaceful. And maybe having Garrett close by would, in the long run, work to her advantage. She kept remembering him—and viewing him still—as some incredible specimen of manhood whose kisses had sent her reeling. A romantic hero of epic proportions who knew how to make a woman feel like a *Wo-man.*

Last night, however, Garrett had done a very good impression of a total doofus. Maybe if she stayed here long enough, she'd realize there was nothing more to him than there was to any other man on the planet, and then she could forget about him and focus on what was really important.

Marrying Lyle and saving Riley Communications from bankruptcy.

With an involuntary groan, Renee rolled over and buried her face in her pillow. Suddenly, the day wasn't nearly as bright and cheerful as it had been during those half-conscious moments immediately after waking. Those moments when a person, if she had a mind to, could fool herself into thinking that everything in her life was going to be hunky-dory, even though, as far as her conscious mind was concerned, she might as well just roll herself over a waterfall in a barrel.

Still, lying in bed groaning wasn't going to improve matters, she thought. So she pushed herself up and slung her feet over the side of the bed, yawned lustily as she unfolded her arms high above her head and...

And immediately halted, mid-gape and mid-stretch. Because her gaze traveled beyond the open bedroom door, through the living room and the windows on the opposite wall, into the great outdoors. And what she saw outdoors was indeed great. Just beyond those windows, Garrett stood shirtless, with leather gloves covering his hands, poised to chop wood.

Now *this,* she decided, was the way to wake up in the morning.

The early morning sun kissed his hair with golden highlights and bathed his body with a warm, wicked glow. The hair scattered over his chest was slightly darker than the thatch of pale brown on his head, gradually arrowing downward to thicken around his navel before dipping below the waistband of his faded blue jeans—which, Renee couldn't help noting, rode dangerously low on his hips. When he gripped the ax, the muscles in his arms flexed and bowed, and Renee swallowed hard in an effort to alleviate the total evaporation of moisture from her mouth.

Good heavens, he was incredible looking. Like a Greek god sculpture. One of the heroes, she decided, Hercules or Pericles. She'd awaken to a manifestation of Garrettcles, God of Beefcake.

She watched, mesmerized, as he swung the ax high over his head and brought it down with a leisurely *thump*, easily splitting a good-size log in two. Then he bent to pick up another, placing it carelessly on the stump before slicing through it in much the same fashion. For a good twenty minutes, Renee sat motionless on the edge of her bed and watched him work, focusing mostly on the corded muscles of his torso that bunched and expanded with every lift of the ax. But she couldn't help noticing, too, the way his arms and body moved steadily, rhythmically, up and down…up and down…up and down…

And totally unbidden, the image of another activity that sent a body up and down exploded in her brain. Before she could stop it, she was assaulted by the thought of a naked Garrett arching atop her own naked form, his body moving in much the same fashion as he made love to her, entering her fiercely again and again and again.

Renee squeezed her eyes shut at the explicit image, but couldn't rout it from her head no matter how hard she tried. Gradually, her arms and body began to tingle, began to tremble, began to heat, and she opened her eyes again. But she was afraid to move, worried that if she budged even an inch in any direction, Garrett would notice the movement and stop what he was doing.

And that simply would not do. Not when she was having

such a nice time watching him. Hey, she was on vacation, she reminded herself. Kate *had* told her to have a good time. So Renee watched Garrett openly and drank her fill of him—well, as much as she dared fill herself with a man like that—and pretended it was all simple fun.

Eventually, though, evidently having chopped enough wood to suit his needs, Garrett did stop working, and Renee tried not to become suicidal over it. By the time he was finished, perspiration glistened on his body, and bits of wood had tangled in the hair on his chest. For a moment, she wondered if she had ever awakened from sleep, because the sight of him was just too dreamy for words.

Cautiously, quietly, she rose from the bed, taking care to move only when Garrett was facing away from the cabin. She wasn't sure how easy it would be for him to look through the windows and see inside, and the last thing she wanted to do was get caught spying on him. Especially dressed in her Pinky and the Brain pajamas.

At one point, when he turned away, she tiptoed through the living room, only to have him quickly turn back. Her movements must have caught his attention. Because like two heat-seeking missiles, his eyes honed in on her, and the fire glittering in his gaze burned her right down to her soul.

And all Renee could think was, *Yikes.*

In spite of the riotous sensations scorching her insides, she lifted a hand and wiggled her fingers in a feeble greeting. The side of Garrett's mouth twitched in response, almost as if he were battling a smile, then he raised a gloved hand in response. She supposed it would be rude to ignore him, so reluctantly she made her way to the front door and went outside.

The morning air was cool and crisp, redolent of pine trees and spring and the earthy aroma of men at work. Although the sun overhead was warm enough, she wrapped her arms around herself. By the time she rounded the side of the cabin, Garrett had shrugged into his denim shirt, but he hadn't bothered to button it. He was still wearing those leather gloves, and he was busily gathering the wood he'd chopped into nice, manageable pieces. He was also, she couldn't help but notice, very, *very* sexy.

And he was ignoring her.

So much for trying to be polite, she thought. Fine. If that was the way he wanted to play it...

Hastily, she spun to return to the cabin, hoping she could pretend the last five minutes had never happened, just like she was trying to pretend last night had never happened. Just as she had been trying for three months to pretend New Year's Eve had never happened. But before she could escape, Garrett called her name, and the sound of it—so soft and sweet and seductive—stopped her dead in her tracks.

"Renee."

It was the first time he'd called her that, and hearing it spoken so roughly, so quietly, so near, set off little explosions in her belly that quickly fireballed to every corner of her psyche.

"What?" she asked.

"Good morning," he said simply.

She glanced over her shoulder but didn't turn around. The sun was behind him, giving the impression that he was the source of its power, its heat, its fire. He was close enough to Renee that she noted for the first time how the highlights in his hair—some of them—were the result of silver as much as gold. And she saw that his eyes, those warm, brandied eyes, were touched with gold at the centers. The musky, early morning scent of him surrounded her, and involuntarily, she inhaled as deeply as she could, holding the air inside her lungs until she began to grow dizzy with it.

"Good morning," she said with a reluctant exhalation of breath.

He pushed past her with an armload of wood, headed for her door. "I expected you to be a late sleeper."

"What time is it?" she asked, surprised that she hadn't noticed the time when she awoke. Normally, the first thing she did upon waking was check the clock. Then again, normally she didn't awaken to the sight of a half-naked man bathed in glorious sunlight just outside her window.

"It's a little past seven," he told her.

She followed him into the cabin and watched as he began to stack the logs by the fireplace. "Is that why you chose now to chop wood right outside the living room window? Because you thought I'd be sleeping late, and this way you could wake me up?"

He straightened and threw her a lazy smile. "Now how could you think I'd be mean enough to do something like that?"

She smiled back, a bit less lazily, she was certain. "Maybe because…that's exactly what you did?"

Slowly, he began to tug off a glove. "Gee, I guess I did. Imagine my embarrassment."

Renee nodded. Yeah, his embarrassment over such a thing would definitely be imaginary, she thought. For some reason, though, she couldn't quite work up the irritation she figured she should be feeling.

"Actually, you and your embarrassment can rest easy," she told him, "because it wasn't you chopping wood that woke me up."

He arched his brows in surprise. "No? What was it then, bad dreams? Doubts about the future? Guilty conscience?"

Strangely, there was no menace, no bitterness in his voice at all. Only a reluctant good humor that made her smile faintly in surprise. She took a few experimental steps into the living room, but was careful to keep the couch between them. "You'd like that, wouldn't you?" she asked him. "Me suffering from bad dreams and such."

"Why would I like that?" he asked her.

"Frankly, I have no idea," she told him honestly. "But I definitely get the impression that you're looking for the worst in me. I just wish I knew why."

His expression changed not one iota at her charge. "I'm not looking for the worst in you," he assured her. "In fact, I'm not looking for anything at all."

She nodded slowly. "Yeah, you know, now that you mention it, I think I can believe that."

"What do you mean?"

She shrugged, feigning indifference. "Just that you seem like the kind of person who gave up on trying to figure out life a long time ago."

He settled his hands on his hips in a gesture she might interpret as boredom, but his face revealed nothing of what he might be feeling. "That's true enough," he told her. "Why try to understand something you can't control?"

"You don't think you can control life?" she asked.

"Nope."

"Really?"

"Really."

"Huh." She eyed him speculatively.

He eyed her warily. "What does that mean?"

"What does what mean?"

"That 'huh' you muttered. What did it mean?" His posture had gone from careless to intimidating in no time flat, and he glared at her with undisguised menace.

Renee hunched her shoulders and told him, "It didn't mean anything. Honest."

But Garrett was clearly not convinced. "It sure as hell sounded like it meant something."

"No, really," she said. "I just think you're a very interesting person, that's all."

"Interesting?" he echoed. "Oh, now that doesn't sound good at all."

"Wh-why not?" she stammered.

"Because a man doesn't like to be called interesting by a beautiful woman, that's why not."

Renee gaped at him. "You think I'm beautiful?"

His posture eased some, becoming skeptical. "Oh, please," he muttered. "Don't tell me that's news."

News? she wanted to shout. *News?* Of course it was news. It was every late-breaking bulletin of global importance that had ever rocked the United States of America. No one had ever called her beautiful before. Well, except her father, of course. But his opinion was just a trifle biased. Renee had always thought herself too ordinary-looking, too soft, too round, to ever be considered beautiful by anyone's standards in this day and age.

But Garrett, of all people, had just told her he thought she was. Now she *really* found him interesting. Not that she would *ever* tell him that again.

For a long moment, they studied each other in silence, neither moving, neither glancing away. Then, slowly, Garrett began to tug the glove from his hand, finger by finger. Something about the action made Renee's mouth go dry, so she conceded the staring match to him and turned her attention to the kitchen.

"You want some tea?" she asked, forcing her feet to move in that direction, praying he would take the hint and let the matter of her dubious beauty drop.

He grimaced, and for a moment she feared he would indeed return to the subject matter that she desperately wanted to flee. Thankfully, he, too, seemed to think those waters were best left unstirred.

"No, thanks," he told her. "I'm strictly a coffee inhaler."

She chuckled, relief bubbling through her at the bland turn the conversation had taken. Blandness. Yes. That was what she would strive for during her stay here at the Final Destination. Blandness was good. Blandness was right. Blandness would keep her sane.

"Coffee has too much caffeine for me. I don't like the thought of being addicted to anything. I pity slaves like you."

"Yeah, we're pretty pathetic," he agreed wryly. "Then again, I've been up since five-thirty myself."

Renee made her way to the galley kitchen. It was tiny but bright, thanks to a huge, arched window over which hung half curtains of the most delicate lace. Over her shoulder, she couldn't help reminding Garrett, *"I'm* on vacation. *I* don't have to get up early if I don't want to."

She had hoped he wouldn't follow her into the kitchen, but

she should have known better. No sooner had she filled the teakettle and turned on the flame beneath it than he filled the doorway and turned on the flame beneath her. And if Renee had thought the kitchen small before, it suddenly became microscopic.

Garrett arced one arm over his head, settling it against the doorjamb, then leaned forward a bit, just, she was sure, to invade her space. The action caused his shirt to fall open, and she had to force herself not to openly ogle him—no easy feat, that. So, deciding that if she *must* look at him—and indeed, she was afraid that she must—she should focus on a part of him that was socially acceptable, she settled her gaze on his face. And she found that he was eyeing her thoughtfully, as if he were pondering something other than the conversation they'd been having.

Sure enough, he changed the subject completely when he asked, "So what exactly do you do out there in the real world that makes you get up during the week?"

Renee nibbled her lip anxiously, crossed her arms over her midsection and shifted her weight from one bare foot to the other. "I, uh... Actually, I'm... That is, I..."

"You do work, don't you?"

She shifted her weight again, stalling. "Well, now, you see, work is one of those relative terms that you could apply to so many things in so many ways, something that means so many things to so many people. There are those who work traditional jobs of the blue or white collar variety to earn their daily bread. Others perform volunteer work in order to feed their souls and make peace with themselves. Then there are the people who view their work as a life's calling, such as philosophers and members of the clergy, and the like, while other people would—"

"You're unemployed, huh?"

She nodded quickly and avoided his gaze. "Yeah. Pretty much."

This time Garrett was the one to shift from one foot to the other before asking idly, "Got any prospects?"

She wasn't sure why he would care, but she replied, "One or two."

His gaze fell to the massive diamond glittering on her left hand, and he nodded slowly. "Well, one, anyway."

Renee reined in her pique at his comment but couldn't quite hold her tongue. "Why do I get the impression that you don't approve of me?"

He shrugged, but there was nothing careless about the gesture. "I can't imagine."

"Funny, but ever since I arrived yesterday, I've gotten the distinct impression that you don't—I don't know—*approve* of me. Which is really weird considering the fact that you barely know me."

He pushed himself away from the doorjamb and settled his hands on his hips. "Maybe I know you better than you think."

"And maybe you don't know me at all."

"I know your type. That's enough."

She gaped at him in confusion before asking, "My type? What's that supposed to mean? I wasn't even aware that I had a type."

On the contrary, she'd been hard-pressed all her life to find someone who felt the same way she did about most things. Thank goodness Garrett had come along to inform Renee of this earth-shattering news that she was a *type*. She must search high and low to the ends of the earth and find the other members of her type, she told herself. And then perhaps they could form a Garrett Fortune fan club.

Or not.

But instead of giving her a straight answer, Garrett glanced at the gloves he held in one hand, then reached behind himself to tuck them into the back pocket of his jeans. And he remained steadfastly silent.

So Renee opened a cabinet to retrieve the box of blackberry tea she'd brought and set it on the counter. As she jerked a bag free, untangled the string, then reached into the cabinet for a cup to drop it into, she focused on her task instead of Garrett and said, "Thanks for cutting wood for me. It wasn't necessary, but thank you. Now, if you don't mind, I'm going to have breakfast. Alone.''

"I still have a few more pieces of wood to bring in.''

"Fine. Bring them in. Then go. Your aunt told me to take it easy while I'm here. She told me to relax. And quite frankly, Mr. Fortune, I can't do either of those things when you're around.''

But instead of doing as she asked—surprise, surprise—he only stood there blocking the kitchen door, watching Renee as warily as a man might watch a snake he was trying to decide was or wasn't poisonous.

Just as the thought materialized in her brain, the teakettle began to hiss and whistle, stirring her from her musing. She snatched it from the burner and filled her cup, then bobbed the tea bag a few times for good measure. And all the while, she felt Garrett's gaze on her back, doubling the heat that already plagued her.

But when she looked up to demand what he was looking at, she found that Garrett had gone.

Garrett didn't get far before his conscience started eating at him. Gradually, his pace slowed, and reluctantly he turned to view Kate's cabin in the early morning light. The way the sun shone through the windows, he could make out Renee's movements as she entered the living room. She seemed to be pacing. Quickly. As if she were a little angry about something. Gee, he bet he could tell what it was in one guess.

Garrett Fortune.

Truth be told, he couldn't exactly blame her. When he'd set off for the cabin that morning, he'd told himself he would be doing a good deed by chopping some wood for Renee, seeing as how there had only been a few sticks left in the bin the night before.

Now, of course, he had to admit that he'd only gone down there to…well, to wake her up. Because he'd wanted to rile her. Because he'd wanted to pick a fight with her. Because he figured that as long as he was fighting with her, he couldn't be wanting her. But he was fast beginning to understand that there wasn't much of anything that would make him stop wanting Renee.

She hadn't reacted to his needling the way he'd expected she would. Oh, he'd riled her, all right. But instead of fighting with him, Renee had calmly invited him to have tea with her, as if she were the Queen of England.

Dammit.

Why couldn't he just ignore her? As she'd pointed out, he barely knew her. They'd shared only about an hour in each other's presence, and a good bit of it had been strained.

Well, except for those few kisses on New Year's Eve. Those hadn't been strained at all. On the contrary, he couldn't recall feeling more relaxed, more complete, more…more right in a long, long time than he had in those few moments of holding Renee close. Which, now that he thought about it, probably went a long way toward explaining why he couldn't ignore her.

Then again, there might be another explanation for his inability to pretend she didn't exist, one that would likewise explain his earlier desire to pick a fight with her. Simply put, Renee Riley reminded him of someone he'd just as soon forget—Marianne. His ex-wife.

Not that the two women shared any physical traits—far from it. Marianne Somerset Fortune Van Meter—she still legally claimed Garrett's name, even though they'd been divorced for coming up on three years—was pretty much Renee's physical opposite in every way. She was tall and willowy where Renee was petite and round, with a fall of white-blond hair that hung to the middle of her back in place of Renee's short, dark curls. And Marianne's eyes were the color of the sky, not the ocean, totally lacking the depth and clarity of Renee's green ones.

But the two women shared other, less tangible, things, not the least of which was a very obvious love of the finer things in life. Renee certainly dressed the part of high society and carried herself with elegance and refinement, just as Marianne had. And her little picnic of the night before attested to her upper crust tastes, as did the massive engagement ring decorating her beautifully manicured finger. She was a lover of fine things.

Just like Marianne.

Garrett spun and started toward the main house, all the while trying to push away the memories of his late but hardly lamented marriage. Unfortunately, thoughts of Renee seemed to be irretrievably linked to thoughts of his ex-wife. And he hadn't been able to stop thinking about Renee for more than three months now. So, inescapably, that brief period of marital miss with Marianne just wouldn't work itself out of his system.

He'd met her at law school. Looking back, he supposed he should have seen the signs of her greediness immediately, because she'd said flat out that she was only studying law to make buckets of money. Then, after they'd dated for a few months, she'd started joking that there was no reason for her to continue with school because, she was going to make *her* fortune by marrying one. He hadn't realized until too late that—to Marianne, at least—it wasn't a joke at all.

They'd waited until after they'd both graduated and passed the bar before marrying. Even so, Garrett honestly hadn't thought much about it when she'd decided not to pursue a career in law. He knew she'd never been truly content with her studies, so he'd assumed she would go back to school to focus on something that would make her happy—photography or literature or education. He had gone on to work for the Fortune Corporation as a legal consultant, as had always been the plan. And Marianne…well, she'd settled into married life. Settled really well.

A little too well.

Because she hadn't done much of anything. Except eat out with her friends. Take tennis lessons and skiing lessons and flower-arranging lessons. Go to parties. Go to luncheons. Go to the hairdresser. Go to the mall.

Certainly Garrett hadn't begrudged her some time to enjoy

herself, to sort things out and make some *serious life choices*—he shuddered involuntarily at yet another thing Marianne had in common with Renee—but he'd thought it wouldn't take her longer than a few months to figure out what she wanted to do with her life. Of course, thinking back on it, after a few months—perhaps even less—she *had* decided what she'd wanted to do. She'd wanted to bleed Garrett dry and enjoy herself immensely at his expense.

Even then, he wouldn't have minded her living a life of leisure, so long as she contributed *something* to their marriage. But that was all there had been for her—leisure. And when Garrett had proposed that maybe it was time they started a family, that having kids, the way they had discussed before getting married, might be the way to go, Marianne's leisure time suddenly disappeared.

She didn't have time to have kids, she told Garrett. She didn't have time to start a family. Her life was far too full, far too busy, far too complicated to add kids to the equation. Unfortunately, Garrett had discovered later, Marianne did have time for an addition to her life—the addition of another man. And once he'd realized what was going on, well… He'd decided it was time to put his foot down.

He sighed heavily as he approached the back door to the big house, swung it open and passed through. Immediately, he was assaulted by the overpowering aroma of coffee left too long on the burner. Good. It ought to be just the way he liked it by now—standing up and dancing the hokeypokey. He trudged the length of the kitchen, filled the cup he'd left in the drainer and slugged back a fortifying swallow, grimacing when he realized he forgot to let it cool.

Great. Now he could add being burned to his Why I Can't Afford to Have Renee Riley Around list.

Then again, he supposed he'd been burned by her long before now. Starting with that all-too-brief embrace they'd shared on New Year's Eve.

"Dammit," he said under his breath. He really, really, really wished he would stop thinking about that. Especially in all that explicit detail that tended to embellish the image.

Fortunately for him, he had a full day ahead. He wasn't going to have a spare minute for anything—and that included mooning over lush brunettes with wide green eyes who slept in pajamas inundated with surreal-looking cartoon mice. With a shake of his head and a sigh of frustration, Garrett went to work.

Six

Renee watched the endless blue sky lazily as she lay on her back at the center of a cool crush of clover a good two miles from Kate's cabin, if her estimation was correct. With her eyes mostly closed and her mind mostly cleared, she inhaled the sweet, crisp Wyoming springtime. Little by little, thoughts of Minneapolis and weddings and obligations ebbed away, and at the very fringes of her conscious mind, she began to remember what was truly important in life.

Every now and then, she opened her eyes for whatever reason—a hawk cried out overhead, the wind tickled her nose, a stiff blade of grass poked through her blue jeans or red corduroy shirt—and every time she did, the sky was a different color. Over the course of an hour—or perhaps a month, she wasn't sure how long she lay there—it went from a pale breath of blue to an imperial azure, then on to a melancholy gray and finally a thick, rich slate.

So fascinated was she by the way the colors shifted and ripened that Renee honestly didn't give much thought to what the changes meant. Not until a cold droplet of water splashed onto her forehead, followed by another, then another, then another, until suddenly she was being pelted by thousands of the little beggers, who showed no sign of going away.

Yet still she lay motionless amid the clover, eyes closed, arms folded beneath her head, because it had been way too long since she hadn't had enough sense to come in out of the rain, and she was rather enjoying her uncharacteristic lack of rationality. Acting responsibly and fulfilling obligations took a lot out of a person. There was no reason she had to behave rationally for the moment, even if it did mean she ended up soaked. It wasn't like there was thunder and lightning to worry about. And it wasn't like anyone was going to see her.

As if cued by the thought, however, she heard the sound of a horse approaching at a none-too-laconic pace, and she realized what folly that last thought had been. Turning her head, she was just in time to see a mounted Garrett crest a faint bump on the landscape. He immediately slowed the horse's canter. He must have noted the splash of red on the green, green grass created by her shirt, but as he drew nearer, Renee did nothing to alter her pose. And although she told herself not to get all mushy over him, she couldn't quite quell the quaking of her heart, the speeding of her pulse or the heat that seeped through her entire body at the sight of him.

She'd never been one of those women who swooned over cowboys, had never been able to figure out what was supposed to be so sexy about some guy in muddy boots and a beat-up hat and ragged jeans and shirts with missing buttons and all that. She preferred a man much more sartorially conscientious, someone who was no stranger to soap and water and who could find his way around the men's fragrances department with no help at all from a woman's guiding hand, thank you very much.

But watching Garrett as he approached, she realized she may have been a bit too hasty in coming to such a conclusion. Because as he dismounted and strode toward her, his lean legs scissoring confidently, his big, capable hands hooked loosely in the reins that led a big, wet horse who smelled, well, like a big, wet horse... As she noted the muddy boots and the faded jeans that molded his strong thighs, and observed the way his buttery flannel shirt clung to the muscles that bunched in his strong arms and shoulders... As she took in the battered straw cowboy hat settled low on his forehead and watched the tiny rivulets of rain stream down the creases in his rough jaws and along the finely chiseled lips...

Oh, my.

Well, suffice it to say that Renee honestly couldn't care less if he ever found his way into the men's fragrances department. As long as he always found his way back to her.

She waited until he halted a few feet away and gazed at her with something akin to disappointment. Then she smiled at him and said, "Gosh, should I have seen this coming or what? Now you're going to ask me if I don't have sense enough to come in out of the rain, aren't you?"

His mouth flattened into a thin line, as if she'd just completely spoiled his opening line. "I think that's kind of unnecessary, don't you? Seeing as how there you lie in the grass, soaking wet, telling me all I need to know."

For some reason, the words rolled off Renee's back as easily as the spring raindrops did. She only sweetened her smile as she asked, "And just when was the last time *you* didn't have enough sense to come in out of the rain, Mr. Fortune, hmm?"

He frowned as he dropped the horse's reins, letting the animal graze freely among the sweet, rain-scented clover. Then he covered the few steps necessary to bring him next to her, dropping his hands to his hips as he towered over her. "Oh, let's see now," he said, "I guess it's probably been at least a good thirty years since I lacked the reasoning needed to decipher a simple dilemma like yours."

She eyed him levelly but continued to smile. "Wow, way back even before I was born, huh? Gee, just how old are you, anyway?"

His scowl darkened. So she broadened her smile.

"I'm *not* old," he told her.

"Well, no, not compared to the age of the universe, I suppose," she mused, wondering what devil had crawled inside her to make her bait him this way.

He gritted his teeth. "I'm thirty-six, all right? Not quite ready for the retirement home."

She widened her eyes in feigned surprise. "Thirty-six?" she gasped. "You mean you were actually *alive* when men first landed on the moon? I can't imagine."

A muscle in his jaw twitched, but he said nothing. So Renee laughed, unable to contain her merriment that he would be so sensitive about something as ridiculous as age. Even if it was *advanced* age. Of course, she kept that to herself.

"I'm only teasing," she said. "You were asking for it, the way you were acting."

"Hey, all *I* did was tell you it's been a while since I haven't had sense enough to come in out of the rain."

The downpour must have waterlogged her brain, she thought. Because for some reason, she didn't want to bicker with Garrett Fortune. Instead, she felt like...well, like playing with him. So, rising up on her elbows, she extended a hand toward him, as if she were silently requesting his help to stand. When he folded his strong fingers over hers, she clasped his hand firmly in hers. But instead of pushing her body off the ground, she tugged on his hand—with all her might.

"Then you're long overdue," she said as she jerked hard enough to pull him to the ground beside her.

She had meant for him to simply drop to his fanny on the wet grass beside her, but his surprise at her action must have caused him to slip or lose his footing. In any event, he fell much harder—much faster—than she'd intended him to. And although he flattened his palms to catch himself, the effort came too late. Instead of landing solidly on his fanny, Garrett fell face first into Renee. Or, more accurately, into Renee's chest.

With one hand splayed open in the grass on one side of her head and one fist on the ground beside the opposite shoulder, he caught himself before he knocked the wind out of her.

However, that didn't keep the air from leaving Renee's lungs in a rapid *whoosh*. Because, although he turned his head at the last possible moment, he still landed with his mouth in a *very* inappropriate place.

Well, inappropriate for a man who hasn't yet made his intentions for a woman known. Then again, considering the heated, predatory glitter that brightened his eyes when his gaze collided with hers, Renee was pretty sure what he was intending to do.

Instead of pressing his mouth to the wet skin revealed at the deeply veed opening of her shirt, however, he pushed himself up on his elbows, looming over her. He didn't move away, though, just up, leaving both forearms planted firmly on either side of her head, his chest pressed intimately to her breasts. Renee tried to quell the ragged rhythm of her respiration, but the effort was useless. Because every time her chest rose, it collided with his, the damp heat of their clothing mingling and seeming to grow hotter with every breath she took.

All Renee could do was stare at him towering over her and try not to swoon at the overwhelming need that coursed through her. Rivulets of rain wound down his jaw as the strong column of his throat worked over a difficult swallow. The fire of desire ignited in his eyes, his lips parted in unmistakable need and…

And, well, there was no way she could remain unaffected by him. Although she didn't know what possessed her, she curled her fingers over the brim of his hat and pulled it from his head, then tossed it to the side. His hair was wet beneath it, and she threaded her fingers through the unruly tresses, smoothing them as she went. Garrett closed his eyes as she performed the gesture, swallowing hard again. When he opened his eyes, the heat that had burned there had exploded, becoming positively incandescent.

"What is it about you?" he asked as he searched her face, looking for she knew not what. His voice was at once rough and ragged, soft and serene. "What is it that makes me feel so… That makes me want to…"

"What?" she demanded when he left the question unfinished, her voice as gruff as his.

But he never completed the thought, only shook his head once, almost imperceptibly. However, his gaze never left hers. She wasn't sure who moved first, whether Garrett began to lower his head or she began to lift hers, but somehow they met halfway. And before he had a chance to pull away, without thinking about what she was doing, Renee roped her arms around his shoulders to pull him closer, curled her hand around his warm nape and tangled her fingers in his wet hair. In response to her silent encouragement, he levered his body more fully over hers, buried the fingers of one hand in her curls then dipped his head toward hers.

As he covered her mouth with his, he wedged one strong leg between her thighs, and she gasped at the intimacy of the gesture. He took advantage of her reaction to slip his tongue inside her mouth for a more thorough taste of her, filling her senses with a delicious awareness of every last inch of him. She went limp at the contact, long enough to moan her satisfaction and drive her fingers more tightly in his hair, long enough to silently urge him closer, to insist on more.

Evidently, it was all the encouragement Garrett needed, because more was what he gave her. Lots more. Before Renee realized what was happening, he had moved his entire body until he was lying fully atop her, his legs between hers, spreading her thighs wider, his flat belly pressing into her pelvis, his groin arching insistently against that most intimate part of her.

A bottle rocket ignited in Renee's midsection, sparking and arcing to burn every sense she possessed. Garrett seemed to surround her, to invade her, to fill her. Over and over again, his tongue penetrated her, tasting her to what felt like the depths of her soul. And all she could do was cling to him— to his damp skin, his heated flesh. Cling to him and want him and silently beg him for more.

The wet clothes that separated them grew hot with the friction of their bodies until Renee was certain steam would rise to surround them. He dipped his head to run his tongue along the bow of her collarbone, nudged open her shirt to taste the soft hollow at the base of her throat. Her fingers fought with his shirttail, pulling it from his jeans, until she could splay her hands over his naked back. The muscles beneath her palms bunched and flexed in response to her touch, and Garrett gripped her shoulders, digging his knees into the grass so that he could push himself more desperately against the feminine heart of her. She felt him swell and ripen against her, and she shuddered at the unleashed power she detected in him.

"Oh, Garrett," she cried softly, burying her face in the warm, damp skin of his neck. She parted her lips to drag openmouthed kisses along the salty column of his throat, nuzzling the rough, wet skin of his jaw. "Oh, please," she whispered, not sure what she was asking him to do, only knowing she wanted him—needed him—to do something quickly. *"Please,"* she echoed, this time with a desperation that surprised even her.

He was about to comply, about to fulfill every fantasy, every wish, every dream, every desire Renee had ever had. She knew he was. She could tell by the way he moved against her— sinuously, seductively, in a way that left no doubt the two of them would soar to the highest destination two people could enjoy. But when she lifted her hand to his hair again, to rake her fingers insistently, possessively through the damp, silky tresses, her engagement ring—the monstrosity that Lyle had handed to her without offering to put it on her finger himself— got caught in a single strand of Garrett's hair.

He went absolutely still at the soft tug, clearly knowing what had caused it. But he didn't lever his body off hers or remove his hands from her shoulders. Slowly, deliberately, he lifted his head to gaze at her, and her breath caught at the disappointment that darkened his eyes. Instinctively, she withdrew, but Garrett tightened his grip to hold her in place.

"Boy, that almost worked," he said, his voice flat. "I was *this* close to believing you really wanted me."

"I do want you." Renee wasn't sure where she found the strength to voice the words, but somehow she knew it was imperative that Garrett understand just how much she had wanted him. Still wanted him. Would want him until the day she died.

"I've wanted you for months," she told him. "Ever since New Year's Eve—maybe even before that. There have been times since Kelly's wedding that I think I've wanted you for my entire life without even knowing who you were."

But he only shook his head and smiled grimly. "It's not me you want," he said. "Not really."

This time Renee was the one to shake her head. "I don't understand," she said softly.

"No, I don't suppose you do. But if I were ten years younger—ten years more foolish—I'd still probably take you up on the offer."

Just like that, all the heat he had generated inside her began to cool. "Garrett, don't," she said softly. "Please don't—"

"But I'm not quite the man I used to be," he interrupted her, "and I'm not the kind of man for you. You need—you want…" He sighed heavily, touching a finger to her damp curls. "Hell, you deserve…" But he never finished what he intended to say. Instead, he concluded, "Guess this was just a wasted effort, huh?"

That remark, more than anything else that had passed between the two of them, sank deep into Renee's soul. Just who did he think he was, suggesting that *she* had been solely responsible for their current situation? Corralling all the indignation she felt—which was no mean feat, considering her indignation could fill a couple of dozen universes at the moment—Renee doubled her fists against Garrett's chest and, with a mighty heave, shoved him off her.

"You're the one who followed me, not the other way around," she said as she jackknifed into a sitting position. "If anyone was making an effort here, it was you. And if anyone was being foolish here, it was me."

She scrubbed her hands over her face and raked her fingers through her hair, then rose to leave. But before she could make a clean getaway, Garrett pushed himself from the ground and circled her wrist with strong fingers.

"What are you talking about?" he asked. "Who says I followed you here?"

She forced a nervous chuckle. "Of course you followed me here. You've been following me around ever since I got here."

He narrowed his eyes at her. "I haven't followed you anywhere."

"Oh, please," she said, regaining some semblance of pride. "Every time I turn around, there you are. All I can do is try to figure out why. There must be *some* reason you keep following me around this way."

His cheeks grew ruddy, and she realized with no small amount of astonishment that she'd embarrassed him. "I have *not* been following you around," he said in a low, level voice.

"Then what are you doing here?" she asked him. "Out in the middle of nowhere? In the rain?"

He uttered an exasperated sound, and she got the feeling that, at the moment, he wished he was anywhere *but* out here in the middle of nowhere in the rain.

"I could ask you the same question," he said. "Just what have you been doing, wandering around out here with nothing to protect you from the elements?"

"I haven't been wandering," she said. "I just felt like taking a little hike. And I know exactly where I am—almost two miles south-southwest of the cabin. As to the elements, well, it's only a little rain. And seeing as how I'm neither salt nor sugar, I won't melt." She jerked her wrist free of his hand and folded her arms across her midsection with much satisfaction. "And your excuse for being here would be…?"

He growled something unintelligible under his breath, then dropped his hands to his hips. With clear reluctance, he spoke. "I was worried about you, all right?"

He was also clearly annoyed, but whether his annoyance stemmed from the fact that he'd just confessed something he hadn't wanted to confess or because he was feeling something he didn't want to feel, Renee couldn't rightly say.

"The power went off in the main house," he continued, "so I came down to the cabin to see how you were faring. And when you weren't there, I became…concerned…that you were out in the weather alone. That maybe you got lost. Or…or hurt."

"Well," she said, trying to ignore the confusing little sizzle of delight that shimmied through her at his revelation. "It was nice of you to be…concerned. But I assure you, there's no need to worry about me. I'm more than—"

"No need to worry?" he repeated. "You just passed a rainstorm out in the middle of a field, and you don't think I should worry about you? What next? Will you be taking swimming lessons in a piranha pool?"

Although the topic under discussion was seemingly inconsequential, she knew they were actually arguing about something far more important. Neither of them was willing, however, to admit just how important. And if Garrett wanted to pretend what had just happened between them hadn't happened at all, Renee was perfectly willing to let him do it. However, that didn't mean she was going to let him get off scot-free.

"No," she said in response to his gruffly offered query. "I already know how to swim. Among other things."

He nodded, but there was no confidence in the gesture at all. "Yeah, well, in spite of your vast knowledge, I feel kind of responsible for you, all right?"

She arched her brows as imperiously as she dared. "Responsible? You? For me? I don't *think* so. The only person responsible for me is me."

"While you're staying at the Final Destination, you're my responsibility," he countered in a voice that brooked no argument. "So you'll excuse the hell outta me now if I don't want to take my eyes off of you until you're safe and sound back at Kate's cabin. God only knows what kind of trouble you could get into between here and there."

Okay, that did it. Seething, Renee placed her hands on her hips, watching as Garrett inflated himself to his full six-foot-plus, two-hundred-pound frame. Why wouldn't men accept the fact that women were capable of looking after themselves? she wondered with a slow shake of her head. Why did they find it impossible to believe that women could survive quite nicely without them? Did they really think they were necessary for a woman's well-being and happiness?

As if.

"Fine," she said, somehow managing to keep her tone civil. "If that excuse suits you, I can certainly overlook its lameness if you can."

He dropped his mouth open in confusion. "Just what the hell is that supposed to mean?"

"Just that if you need an excuse like that to make you feel better about the fact that you can't keep your eyes—or your hands—to yourself whenever I'm around, then I'm certainly not going to dissuade you of the notion. You know better than I do what kind of stories you need to tell yourself to make yourself feel better about being attracted to someone."

"*Attracted?*" he exclaimed. But the word seemed to get stuck in his throat, because he began to cough. A lot.

Renee only folded her arms over her midsection and lifted her nose haughtily into the air. "Fine. You don't find me attractive, even if you *did* call me beautiful just yesterday." She rushed on with a smile before he had a chance to communicate. "You only followed me out here—again—because you were concerned about my welfare—again. And you only kissed me—again—because you can't stand the sight of me. Is that it?"

"What's all this 'again' business."

"Just that last night, you had to show me the way to Kate's cabin—which was barely a stone's throw from the main house—because you were *concerned* that I might not be able to find it. And then this morning," she continued before he had a chance to object, "you came down to chop wood for me because you were *concerned* that I didn't have enough. Now I find you following me on my walk, because you're *concerned* that I might get wet. And as for what happened on

New Year's Eve and just a minute ago, well *you* were the one who—"

"So what's your point?" he interrupted before she had a chance to put voice to the profound sharing of souls—not to mention body parts—they'd enjoyed not once, but twice.

"So my point is…" She expelled a restless, anxious sound. "Dammit, Garrett, I'm perfectly capable of handling a little rain, finding a cabin at sunset and chopping my own wood and—"

"You? Chop wood?"

"And it makes no difference to me if you want to use all those things as excuses to cover up the fact that you just want to spend time with me. Admit it. You can't get New Year's Eve out of your mind, can you? God knows you've brought it up often enough."

"Once," he interjected, extending one long index finger into the air. "I brought it up one time. You, on the other hand, have brought it up twice. So who really can't forget who around here, hmm?"

She ignored him and continued with what even she knew was an outrageous bluff. In a tone dripping with too much sweetness, too much sincerity, she asked, "Have you been pining for me all this time? Lying awake in bed at night wondering where I am and what I'm thinking about? Being…*concerned* about me? Oh, Garrett, that is just *so sweet.* Why didn't you tell me how much you cared about me?"

He set his hands on his hips and eyed her thoughtfully, intensely, for a long time before replying. And when he finally did, he said the strangest thing. "Would it have made a difference if I had?"

Renee blinked at him, and suddenly, the bluff she'd been playing with him didn't seem like a bluff at all. "A difference? How? With what?"

He dipped his head toward the massive diamond on her left hand that, even under a cloudy sky, winked brilliantly. "In your engagement. Would you still have told the guy yes?"

She opened her mouth in astonishment, completely at a loss

how to answer. Time seemed to come to a standstill in spite of the light spatter of rain that still fell. And then Garrett laughed, a fakey, gotcha-last, kind of laugh that was in no way convincing. Then he turned and made his way to his grazing horse, effortlessly mounted the animal and, with a quick tug on the bridle, cantered easily away.

Nightfall, as usual, came quickly to the Final Destination. And it came completely, too, seeing as the power outage from the afternoon's storm had yet to be corrected. Garrett stood in his kitchen in the darkness, staring out the window at the silhouette of Kate's cottage stark—and dark—against the night sky.

Well, not entirely dark, he noted. A glimmer of pale light flickered in the living room, telling him that Renee had probably built a fire and lit a candle or two to combat the darkness. But that wasn't what he was seeing as he gazed out the window. Not surprisingly, in his mind's eye, what he was seeing was Renee Riley.

Wet.

Soaking, sexy wet, with her clothes clinging to her like a second skin and leaving absolutely nothing to the imagination. Beneath her man-style corduroy shirt—a garment Garrett told himself no man in his right mind would *ever* find erotic—she hadn't been wearing a bra. Or anything else, for that matter. He'd known because the soaked fabric had hugged the lush curves of her breasts and the taut, ripe outline of her nipples.

He squeezed his eyes shut at the memory, but that didn't stop the ripple of desire that wound through him. Nor did it stop the heat pooling in his groin when he recalled the way her wet blue jeans had hugged her legs—surprisingly long legs for a woman who wasn't particularly tall—with loving familiarity, telling him everything he needed to know about the elegant musculature of her thighs.

And it had been pretty doggone elegant musculature.

Her hair—which he wouldn't have thought could be any wilder than it already was—had been a shimmering, quivering mass of silk the color of bittersweet chocolate, and he hadn't been able to help himself when he'd reached out to wind a few of the unruly curls around his fingers. He hadn't been able to help himself when he'd slowly guided his hand through her hair to cup his palm over the back of her head. He hadn't been able to help himself when he'd pushed her forward, little by little, until her mouth lay right beneath his.

And he hadn't been able to help himself when he'd tried to consume her with one big bite.

He groaned at the memory and drove both hands through his hair, gritting his teeth against the injustice of it all. Renee Riley was a kid, he reminded himself. An *engaged* kid. An engaged kid who was far better suited to a cushy life-style.

Although, now that he thought more about that, Garrett was beginning to wonder if maybe he was being a bit too hasty in making that particular assessment about her character. This afternoon, when he'd put a stop to what he'd just *known* would be a vastly satisfying foray into the soft depths of Renee Riley, his impulse had stemmed more from his shock at finding himself losing control than it had his suspicions about her motives.

But he'd had hours to reflect on that brief little visit to the Magic Kingdom of Erotica, and he was starting to question the reasoning behind his reactions to Renee. Maybe, he thought, his real reason for being wary of her *wasn't* that she might be a fortune hunter. Maybe the real reason he felt cautious was that she was the first woman to come along in a long, long time who made him want to throw caution to the wind and react without thinking.

Ever since New Year's Eve, his behavior around her had been totally unlike him, totally unfathomable. He had been acting without thinking, doing things simply because he *wanted* to do them and not because he thought they were a good idea.

And that frankly terrified him. Because Garrett Fortune was nothing if not a thoughtful, farsighted individual. He'd learned his lesson with Marianne. You don't do something just because it feels good, or right. Because if you do, you wind up getting hurt. Ever since his marriage had gone to hell in a handbasket, Garrett had made sure to give every single action serious consideration before undertaking it. He always had to think things through completely, ponder every possible result of his behavior, before he allowed himself to move.

With Renee, however, consideration, thoughtfulness, ponderings…they'd all gone right out the window. Since this afternoon, however, Garrett had allowed himself the luxury of indulging in all those things again. And he'd come to some mighty interesting conclusions when he'd sat down to think things through.

Because he'd forced himself to remember the fact that Renee was a friend of his aunt Kate's, so chances were good that she traveled in his aunt's social circle. And if that were the case, then it was likely that Renee came from a moneyed family. Therefore, chances were good that she was already rich. Maybe, just maybe, she wasn't a gold-digging opportunist in search of a sugar daddy, after all.

Which, now that Garrett thought *more* about it, meant there was also a good chance that she was engaged because she was in love with the guy who'd given her that big ol' chunk of hardened carbon even if she had shared in a heated exchange of oral exploration with him earlier. Sometimes flesh won out over the heart. Maybe Garrett turned her on physically, but that didn't mean she couldn't be in love with someone else. Stranger things had happened.

Yet for some reason, the realization that Renee might genuinely care for the man she was supposed to marry was even more distasteful to Garrett than the money-grubbing one had been. Because money grubbing he could deal with, and had, on more than one occasion. Marianne wasn't the only woman of his acquaintance who'd seen dollar signs instead of cupid's darts where Garrett was concerned. But love…

Well, now, that was a tricky one. He'd never really been in love. He'd told himself, at the time, that what he'd felt for Marianne was love, but she'd been remarkably easy to get over once their marriage had ended. Sure, he was still angry about the whole thing, but he felt more foolish than he did anything else. So he couldn't rightly say he'd ever really been in love with his ex-wife, even when she was his wife.

But Renee, now, she might just be in love with the man she'd promised to marry. And if that were the case...

Well, if that were the case, there was really no point in standing at the window gazing at Kate's cabin and wanting to howl at the moon, was there? Then again, when he remembered the way Renee had responded to him that afternoon, the way she'd opened wide to bid him entry... Well, then. Maybe she wasn't as deeply in love as a woman ought to be when she's about to make a lifelong commitment to a man.

Then again, why did he care?

Frustrated at the winding, unending path of his thoughts, Garrett spun away from the window and stared at the dark kitchen instead. He cared because Renee Riley turned him on something fierce, that was why. He cared because something inside him—something earthy, unmanageable and hot—responded to something equally volatile in her. He cared because he couldn't stop thinking about her. And something told him he wasn't likely to stop thinking about her just because she put on a white wedding dress and said "I do" to another man.

He only wished he knew if doing that would make a difference in her feelings for him.

Because she did have feelings for him—he could tell that by the hungry look that had exploded in her eyes when he'd asked her if it would have made a difference in her engagement if he'd told her long ago that he'd been pining for her. He just wished he could tell if those feelings went beyond the physical.

And there was really no point in denying it to himself any longer—he *had* been pining for Renee ever since New Year's Eve. Maybe not in the poetic, overly romantic sense she had implied in her teasing question that afternoon, but he had been pining for her. At least, his body had been pining for her body. Maybe the attraction between them really was nothing more than a physical phenomenon. Maybe it was Mother Nature stepping in to play a joke, that was all.

Then again, maybe it wasn't.

Still, there was no reason they couldn't explore that attraction, was there? Renee wasn't married yet.

A devil took hold of Garrett as he thought about that, and he felt a wicked smile curl his mouth. Maybe he ought to mosey on up to Kate's cabin and offer Renee an apology for his behavior earlier in the day. And maybe he ought to take a little peace offering when he went. And seeing as how she had such highfalutin' tastes, it might not be a bad idea to venture into the wine cellar—deep in the wine cellar, where he kept the really good stuff—so the two of them could enjoy a little refreshment with their candlelight as he apologized.

Because suddenly, Garrett wanted very badly to apologize to Renee. Mainly because he was interested to see how she would accept his apology. And if things went the way he hoped…

He let his mind wander off into the sublime for a moment, and his smile grew more wicked. Well, then. Maybe Renee would be making a few alterations to her wedding plans. Maybe she'd see—as he did—that, sometimes, you just couldn't fight what fate had in store for you. And, sometimes, what fate had in store for you had absolutely no similarity to what you had planned for yourself. Sometimes, fate could be a little tricky.

Funny thing, fate was. You just never knew where it would take you…

Seven

"**I** thought you might be running low on snacks by now."

Renee gaped at the man standing at the front door and waited for a punch line, because surely this was just a joke, right? What else could explain the appearance of Garrett Fortune looking freshly showered, dressed in a pair of baggy, cognac-colored corduroy trousers and a dark blue sweater, accessorized by a way-too-sexy grin, a flashlight and what appeared to be a...picnic basket?

She glanced at her attire and was thankful for the power outage, because her ensemble was decidedly less appropriate for visitation—black drawstring sweatpants and a voluminous white, long-sleeved, scooped-neck tunic of similar fabric. Accessorized by thick, white athletic socks, her outfit was the picture of vacation slobbery.

And suddenly, for some odd reason, Renee wished that she had packed something a little less slobbery. Like maybe one of those filmy lace teddies, the kind she'd never bought because she suspected they itched something awful, but she'd always wondered if maybe, in the long run, you didn't care that they itched because you didn't have them on that long, anyway.

Not that Renee was a big expert on revealing lingerie, but seeing she was about to become a married woman, she might do well to buy one or two articles of the negligee persuasion. Of course when she reminded herself that it would be Lyle, not Garrett, who'd be seeing her in such outfits, her sudden shopping spree didn't seem quite so pressing anymore.

And who did she think she was, anyway, entertaining such galloping thoughts—about lingerie, no less—in front of Garrett Fortune?

"Renee?"

The sound of her name uttered in that rough, masculine voice jarred her from her bizarre musings, and she shook her head quickly to clear it. Unfortunately, those bizarre musings refused to clear completely, because all she could keep thinking about was being scantily clad with Garrett Fortune.

Oh, dear.

"What?" she replied, still marveling at his appearance, barely recognizing her own voice in that quietly uttered word. Since when did she sound so much like Kathleen Turner?

"Are you okay?" he asked, softly enough to pull her gaze to his face.

Ooh, bad idea.

Because his face, like the rest of him, was way too yummy for her comfort. He'd obviously just shaved, because his skin was smooth and ruddy and fragrant, and his eyes... She bit back the sigh that always bubbled up whenever she gazed too deeply into Garrett's eyes. His eyes were the color of brandy, and every bit as intoxicating. And at the moment, they were lit with something she dared not contemplate for too long.

"I'm fine," she lied. "What are you doing here?"

He lifted the picnic basket, lowering the flashlight's beam onto it for her inspection. "I thought you might be out of snacks by now," he repeated. "I noticed you didn't go anywhere in your car today."

She hunched her shoulders a little anxiously. "No, it was too nice a day to leave the ranch."

"It rained," he reminded her.

Not that Renee needed a reminder. She'd spent the better part of the afternoon lying on the couch with her eyes closed, replaying in her heated imagination every erotic caress the two of them had shared.

"I know," she said, "but I like rain."

He chuckled, a low, lascivious rumble of sound. "Yeah, I could tell."

"Besides," she added, "I really did bring plenty of food. Thanks, but I'm doing okay."

She waited to see if he would take the hint, the hint being that he should please, for the love of God, leave now, before she hauled him inside and made a snack out of *him*. But instead of saying goodbye, he only smiled at her. He *got* the hint, all right, she could tell that quite plainly. He just wasn't going to *take* it.

As if to illustrate, he asked, "Can I come in?"

She opened her mouth to tell him no—truly she did—but what came out was, "Sure, I guess so."

Still, she couldn't quite bring herself to step aside. Garrett, however, felt no hesitation, because he took a step forward, an action that brought him barely a breath away from Renee. So naturally, she reacted the way any other red-blooded woman would react. She bolted into the cabin as quickly as she could.

She wasn't sure, but she thought she heard him chuckle before he closed the door. And then, with a soft, almost indiscernible click, he and Renee were closed off from the rest of the world. The living room was lit by the fire and half a dozen strategically placed candles by which she'd fruitlessly been trying to read. There was enough light for them to get around fairly easily, but not enough for her to feel comfortable being alone with Garrett.

Why had he come down here? she wondered. Had he really just wanted to make sure she had enough to eat? Or had he been motivated by a hunger of an altogether different nature? Because although she did have plenty of food to eat, Renee hadn't quite felt sated since arriving at the Final Destination. And after that puzzling, albeit wildly frenzied, encounter earlier in the day, she couldn't help wondering if maybe Garrett had been suffering from a similar problem.

She spun to face him just as he moved up behind her and found herself standing nearly toe to toe with him. He was so tall, she thought, especially when she was standing in her stocking feet this way. Thankfully, he mumbled a soft, "Excuse me," and stepped around her, moving to the other side of the sofa. He deposited the picnic basket on the coffee table, where the remains of her dinner still sat.

"I see you *do* have enough to eat," he said when he took in what was left of the pickled herring and crackers, the black olives and green grapes. "But you seem to be running low on wine. How about a refill?"

Before she could reply, he tipped the half-full bottle of Beaujolais over her glass until it was three-quarters full. Then he deftly extracted a glass for himself from the basket and emptied the remaining contents of the bottle into it. Before setting the bottle down, he turned the label toward the firelight to inspect it.

"Rothschild, 1987," he said, obviously impressed by the selection. "You really do have excellent taste."

From the way he voiced it, though, Renee wasn't sure she should take his observation as a compliment. "Twelve years of etiquette schooling does have its benefits, I suppose."

He arched his eyebrows in surprise as he placed the empty bottle on the table and lifted his glass. "You went to etiquette school?" he asked before sampling the wine.

"Gee, you mean it doesn't show?" she asked.

He swallowed, then laughed again. "Well, now that you mention it…"

She frowned before replying dryly, "Yeah, well, even etiquette school can only teach so much tolerance."

He dipped his head in acknowledgment of her barb. "Touché,'' he said softly. ''Which provides a nice segue for my explanation as to why I came down here.''

She feigned indifference, in spite of the way her heart began to hammer hard behind her rib cage. And because she suddenly needed something to do with her hands, she bent to retrieve her wineglass, curling her fingers around the bowl with what felt like enough force to shatter it.

Nevertheless, she somehow managed to sound bland as she asked, ''And that would be why?''

He returned her gaze levelly. ''I came because I feel like I owe you an apology.''

It was the last thing Renee expected Garrett Fortune to say. He didn't even seem like the kind of man who would admit he had erred, let alone apologize. But before she could comment, he began to talk again, in that soft murmur of a voice she'd found so incredibly seductive on New Year's Eve.

''You're right,'' he went on, ''I haven't been the most tolerable person since you arrived yesterday. I really don't have any excuse for that, save to say that I have a lot on my mind. Still, that's no excuse at all, is it? Consider this—'' he gestured toward the basket ''—a little peace offering. I promise I'll try to behave myself from now on.'' Still watching her closely, he lifted the glass to his lips again.

Renee honestly didn't know what to say. Although she hadn't exactly enjoyed sparring with Garrett, for some reason, it seemed preferable to being amiable with him. At least when they were annoying each other, she didn't have to worry about being attracted to him. Well, not *too* attracted, anyway. Not much. Not really.

But making peace… For some reason, that was a bit scary. The last thing she needed was to be comfortable with him, because that could only lead to trouble. Not that she could ever truly feel comfortable around him. Not as long as he roused such a bewitched, bothered and bewildered reaction from her.

''Well, my goodness, Mr. Fortune,'' she finally said, breaking what had started to become an awkward silence. "You seem to have manners, after all."

"One or two," he confirmed. "Most folks just don't know where to look for them. And knock off the 'Mr. Fortune' stuff. Call me Garrett."

She nodded, telling herself to look at something—anything—else in the room. But, not surprisingly, she found that she simply could not look away. The way the firelight played over his face—first casting his features in darkness, then in dancing light—hid whatever he might be thinking. And she found herself wanting very badly to figure him out.

So she asked, "Just what wondrous work of magic did I perform to bring your manners to the fore?"

He threw her a lazy smile and lifted his glass to his lips for a lengthy taste, rolling the wine around in his mouth for a moment before swallowing. Then, his eyes never leaving hers, very, very quietly, he said, "You got wet."

For just a few seconds, Renee's heart seemed to stop beating. Then, as if it wanted to make up for lost time, it began to thunder three times faster than usual. "I...I got...I got *what?*" she stammered, certain she must have misunderstood him.

But instead of repeating or clarifying himself, Garrett threw her another lazy smile and filled his mouth with wine. So, pretending she hadn't heard a thing, Renee sipped her wine, slowly and fastidiously, and wondered what he was wearing that made him smell so good.

"So when are you getting married?" he asked when he'd swallowed.

Oh, good, Renee thought. Something to take her mind completely off romance. Her wedding to Lyle. Funny, though, how much different she felt when she was reminded of the event. Before, recalling her impending wedding had always made her feel nauseous. But now, suddenly, the reminder made her feel very, very sad.

Trying not to sound too halfhearted when she answered, she told him, "In a little under a week."

Garrett had just taken another sip of his wine, and something about her response must have surprised him, because he suddenly began to cough as if he were choking. Badly. "A week?" he finally sputtered feebly. "You'll be married in one week?"

She nodded. "Yes. Is there a problem?"

When he continued to cough, she took a few cautious steps toward him, then patted him on the back a couple of times to see if it might help him clear his lungs. What she encountered, though, was solid steel beneath her fingertips. There was little chance any patting she did registered below all those acres of muscle.

Nevertheless, he must have felt the gesture, because he immediately quit coughing and wiped the side of his hand over his mouth. Then he continued to study her with a hard, heated gaze. "But...one week?" he repeated, his voice rougher than she'd ever heard it. "That's...that's only a week away."

At the fire glittering in his eyes, Renee quickly pulled her hand back, fearing she might be burned if she didn't. "Um, yeah. It is. So?"

He expelled an exasperated sound. "So it's just that... I mean..." He blew out another one of those irritated expulsions of air, then said, "So I didn't think you were engaged when we...on New Year's Eve, I mean."

Renee dipped her head to gaze into her glass as she said, "I wasn't engaged then."

"So this was one of those whirlwind courtships?"

"No," she replied honestly, still not looking at him.

He waited for her to elaborate, and when she didn't, he asked, "Have you known this guy long?"

Renee really wished they could talk about something else. But Garrett clearly wasn't going to let the subject drop until she'd told him everything he wanted to know. So, with a sigh of resignation—surely that wasn't wistfulness in the sound—she told him, "I met him last November, at a party."

"And you've been engaged since when?"

"Since the end of January."

Garrett hesitated, as if he were still waiting for an explanation. But seeing that Renee didn't have one to give him, she remained silent.

So he continued, "Then it *was* one of those whirlwind courtships."

She wanted to deny it, wanted to tell him there really hadn't been a courtship at all, that her marriage was little more than a business arrangement. But she kept her mouth firmly shut, because she feared such a revelation might open the door to something she had no business inviting into her life. She only stood silently staring into her wine, refusing to look at Garrett lest she reveal way too much.

"You must really love him." He offered the observation in a flat, toneless voice.

Renee said nothing in response.

"He must be very special to you."

Still she remained silent.

"I certainly hope he appreciates what he's getting."

Renee couldn't help but smile sadly at that, especially since there wasn't an ounce of affection in Garrett's voice when he uttered the comment. "Oh, I think he does," she said softly. "In his own way."

There was another moment of awkward silence, then Garrett asked, "Is it anybody I know?"

Renee sighed deeply again and forced herself to look at him. When she did, she found him staring at her with a mixture of confusion and anger and...and something else she really didn't think she should contemplate.

"I imagine you do know him," she said. "Everyone who's ever set foot in Minneapolis seems to know him. I'm engaged to... That is, the man I'm marrying is..." She sighed, unwilling, for some reason, to put voice to her fiancé's name. When Garrett continued to gaze at her expectantly, however, she said softly, "Lyle Norton. I'm engaged to Lyle Norton."

The expression on his face told Renee Lyle was the last man Garrett might have expected her to name. His voice was ripe with skepticism when he said, "Lyle Norton? Are you serious?"

She nodded. "You sound like you don't believe me."

"No, it's not that. Just—"

"What?"

He lifted one shoulder and let it drop in a gesture so quick, she wasn't sure it could even qualify as a shrug. "I've met Lyle. On a couple of occasions, as a matter of fact."

"And?"

Another quick rise and fall of that shoulder. "And...I don't know. He seems like a nice enough guy, I guess. A little too consumed with his work, maybe, but still a nice guy."

"He is a nice guy," she agreed halfheartedly.

Garrett nodded. "Good-looking cuss."

"Yes, he is that."

"Smart."

"Very."

"Ambitious."

"Extremely."

"Rich."

"That, too."

"Young." Garrett practically spat that word, as if Lyle's age made him a serial killer.

"He's twenty-six, three years older than me," Renee said, wondering where the conversation was leading. Voicing her thoughts, she asked, "What does any of this have to do with anything?"

"You tell me," he said softly.

There was something unmistakably seductive in his voice, but for the life of her, Renee couldn't say what it was or why it was there. Striving for a light tone she didn't come close to feeling, she said, "Look, you're the one who's making a big deal out of my engagement to Lyle. I'd just as soon talk about something else."

He nodded sharply. "Yeah, I bet you would."

She narrowed her eyes. "What's that supposed to mean?"

"Just that it seems kind of funny, you hiding out in the

wilds of Wyoming this way, less than a week before your own wedding."

She gaped at him. "Who says I'm hiding out?"

"The only reason Kate ever sends anyone up to this cabin," Garrett said adamantly, "is because they need a place to hide out."

"Th-that's ridiculous," Renee stammered, cursing herself for the uncertainty she heard in her voice. "I'm only going to be here for a few days. Why would I be…hiding out?"

"Good question," he replied as he took a step toward her. "Got a good answer?"

"I don't need a good answer. I'm not hiding out," she insisted as she took a step backward in retreat. "I'm…I'm vacationing. That's all. Taking a few days off to recuperate from the wedding plans."

"Vacationing?" he echoed, clearly not buying it. And, much to her dismay, he took another step toward her. "A week before your wedding? Call me uninformed, but isn't that honeymoon thing that comes immediately after a wedding supposed to be something of a vacation? For the bride *and* the groom?"

Unable to tolerate his nearness—boy, he smelled good—Renee spun around and made her way to the couch. She sat down, tucked her feet underneath her and gently placed her wine on the coffee table. "Lyle and I aren't taking a honeymoon," she said, surprised she could deliver the information without feeling the irritation she figured she should probably feel over something like that. Still, at least it gave her a plausible—well, sort of plausible—excuse for why she'd be visiting Kate's cabin now.

Garrett followed her example and moved to sit at the opposite end of the sofa, depositing his glass directly beside hers. But where Renee had pretty much curled herself into a protective little ball when she sat down, Garrett opened himself up. He stretched one arm along the back of the couch, then settled the other on the armrest beside him. And seeing as it wasn't a very big sofa—a love seat, really—that meant he was way too close for comfort. Close enough that he could reach right out and touch her if he wanted to.

And, evidently, he did want to. Because he dropped his hand to skim it along the top of her shoulder just shy of her shirt as he asked, "Why aren't you taking a honeymoon?"

The brush of his fingertips along her bare flesh went far enough to move the wide, scooped neck of her tunic over her shoulder, exposing more than a hint of creamy skin. Renee's first instinct was to reach up and cover herself again, but she worried that if she did, Garrett would notice the action. Right now, his gaze was focused on her face—maybe he hadn't even realized her shirt had shifted. The last thing she wanted to do was draw attention to the fact.

Unfortunately, even with his gaze locked with hers, he seemed to notice immediately, because he dropped his fingers lower, rubbing his thumb gently over her collarbone. Renee's heart began to beat double time, sending blood crashing through her veins to heat parts of her that in no way needed warming. Even though he was barely touching her, she felt her body come alive in places she'd never known could feel. And although she knew she should tell Garrett to stop, she couldn't quite find the words or the strength—or the desire—to do so.

What was the harm? she asked herself. It was just a little caress, nothing to be so concerned about. He probably wasn't even paying attention to what he was doing. She'd look silly if she told him to stop touching her, might even embarrass him.

Besides, it really did feel nice....

So she sighed heavily and tried to remember what they had been talking about. Her honeymoon. Right. Discussing that ought to dispel any trace of sexual desire she might be feeling.

"Lyle," she began, but her voice squeaked on his name, as if she were having trouble saying it. So she tried again, with rather mixed results. "Um, Lyle," she said, trying to focus on her fiancé, instead of the man who really commanded her attention. "He, uh...he couldn't work a honeymoon into his schedule. He has to leave again on a business trip the day after our wedding.''

"Again?'' Garrett echoed absently. "Why again?''

Renee swallowed hard in an effort to slow her rapid pulse, to no avail. Because her heart rate only seemed to triple. "He, uh, he's on a business trip now, too, and won't be home until the day before the wedding.''

The fingers skimming along her collarbone and shoulder paused in their exploration as, with deceptive idleness, he dropped his gaze to his hand. After a moment, his fingers began to glide along her bare flesh again, this time widening the distance to include her shoulder and the base of her throat—and all points in between.

"You mean he's flying in for one day to marry you, then flying right back out again?'' Garrett asked. "That's not very nice of him.''

Renee plucked at a nonexistent piece of lint on her sweat-pants and tried to pretend that Garrett's touch wasn't turning her into a mass of quivering, overheated Jell-O. "Lyle is, uh, a, um… He's a very busy man,'' she finally managed to say.

Garrett continued to strum his fingers along her shoulder, back and forth…back and forth…back and forth… But he seemed not to notice how rattled she was becoming from the simple touch. He continued to watch the motion of his hand dancing along her flushed skin as he said very quietly, "The man must be *awfully* damned busy to leave a woman like you alone when he could be…enjoying you.''

Renee tried to steady her breathing for a moment, then abandoned the effort, recognizing it as fruitless. Somehow, she managed a small smile as she said, also very quietly, "You know, I'm not sure, but I think you just paid me a compliment.''

His fingers paused in their gentle caressing as he lifted his gaze to meet hers. The firelight rioted in his hair, gilding the short, silky tresses with gold and copper, and warmed his face as if the heat came from within him. Renee's heart began to hammer in that rough, irregular rhythm again, and little explosions detonated throughout her entire body.

"Why shouldn't I compliment you?" he asked, his gaze never leaving hers. "There's a lot about you worth complimenting."

Oh, this was definitely a conversation she shouldn't be having, Renee told herself. Because suddenly, her wedding date was looking more like an execution date.

Growing more flustered with every passing second, she blurted, "Are you flirting with me?"

He chuckled low, the most tempting sound Renee had ever heard in her life, then brushed his fingertips along the line of her bare shoulder again. But instead of repeating the action in the opposite direction, he dipped his middle and index fingers gently into the hollow at the base of her throat.

And he rested them there as he said, "Nope. I figure I got past flirting this afternoon."

Surely, he could hear the pounding of her heart now, Renee thought. There could be no mistaking the way it thundered between her breasts. "This afternoon?" she said, her voice barely a whisper. "You call that flirting? Boy, you have a lot to learn about flirting."

The fingers at the base of her throat dipped to her breastbone, then began to follow it, moving toward the scooped neckline of her shirt. Slowly, slowly…lower, lower…until his hand rested at the source of the dusky valley between her breasts.

"Sweetheart," he said in that maddeningly smooth voice, "I've forgotten more about flirting than you'll ever know in your lifetime. One thing I do recall, though, is that it's generally a waste of time. When you get to my advanced age, you realize just how precious a commodity time is. And you learn not to waste it."

For some reason, Renee wanted to cry out, *Then what are you waiting for?* But she checked herself in time. Even so, she couldn't think of a single other thing to say. Which was just as well, because Garrett clearly wasn't finished with her yet. He pinned her with his gaze, and even in the pale glow of the firelight, she could see his pale brown eyes flashing fire, his lips parting slightly, as if he couldn't quite get enough air.

And all Renee could do was wait. For what, she couldn't have said. But there was a sizzle of anticipation crackling through her body that was unmistakable.

"Your heart is racing," he said in that level, oh, so silky voice. "I can feel it beneath my fingertips. Why is your heart pounding like that, Renee?"

She swallowed with some difficulty. "Why do you think?"

He flattened his hand, spreading it wide-open over her heart. The action splayed his fingers out over part of her breast, a gesture that did nothing to slow the telltale raging of her pulse, and everything to enhance it.

"I don't know," he said. But the smile that curled his mouth told her he knew exactly why. "You'll be getting married in a week. I can't think of a single reason you'd be sitting here with me, all alone in the dark, your heart racing like a thoroughbred out of the gate."

His hand against her bare flesh seemed to sear her. But as much as Renee told herself to move away or to brush his hand aside, she felt paralyzed by his very presence, completely unable to look away from his face. "Oh, can't you?" she finally asked.

"Well, maybe I can think of one reason," he replied, his voice dropping even lower. "Maybe the reason your heart is pounding so hard is because…I turn you on."

Oh, my, Renee thought, her blood galloping even faster at his total certainty about what was the source of her raging pulse. She supposed there was little point in denying his charge, seeing as he had all the evidence he needed right there in the palm of his hand. Nevertheless, she said, "Or maybe it's because…" She sighed brokenly. "Because you scare me."

He nodded slowly, his eyes never leaving hers as he murmured, "Maybe I do. Because maybe your response to me is telling you more than you want to know about your response to your husband-to-be.''

Okay, Renee thought, the time had come to put some distance between herself and Garrett. With no small effort, she broke her gaze from his, scooped up her wineglass and strode quickly to the fireplace. The flames snapped and leaped in response to the swiftness of her movement, and she felt its heat flare against her body.

At least, she thought it was the fire's heat she felt. Because surely Garrett wouldn't continue to affect her so, not when there was the distance of half a room between them. Unsure what to do with her hands—other than run them all over his glorious body, at least—she lifted her glass to inhale a fortifying taste of her Beaujolais. And when that didn't even come close to soothing her nerves or ordering her thoughts, she raised the glass again for another taste. Followed by another. And then another. And another.

''Whatever response I may have to you,'' she finally said when the glass was empty, bothered by the fact that Garrett had yet to comment on her abrupt flight from the couch, not to mention her sudden, unquenchable thirst, ''it's nothing like what I feel for Lyle.''

Well, that was certainly true, she thought. Still, there was no reason she had to clarify things for him, was there?

He hadn't altered his pose on the sofa save to turn his head to look at her, but he rose and slowly covered the distance between them, taking a position at the fireplace much like her own. Except that his position was much taller, much broader and far more intimidating.

''So you're saying you don't feel a response to me?'' he asked idly.

Renee shook her head. ''Um, no. No, of course not.''

''No, you don't feel a response to me?'' he asked. ''Or no, that's not what you're saying, that you *do* feel a response to me. A really big one, judging by the way you're looking at me right now.''

Renee felt heat rise into her cheeks, and she swallowed with some difficulty. "I—I'm saying that I don't feel a response to you," she stammered. She waited a moment to see if a bolt of lightning would strike her dead for telling such a blatant lie. Strangely, none did. Heartened by the lack of retribution, she continued, "Other than marveling at your amazing arrogance, I mean."

He widened his eyes in what was obviously feigned surprise. "Arrogant? Me?" he asked innocently.

"Arrogant. You," she replied. "What else would you call a man who considers himself so irresistible?"

He smiled, a toe-curling, heart-stopping smile that hit her right square in the libido. "But, Renee, sweetheart," he said quietly, "I *am* irresistible."

She did manage to laugh at that, albeit nervously. "Arrogant, with a vivid imagination to boot," she said, proud of herself for commanding such a light tone of voice.

"Imagination," he repeated. "Is that what it is?"

She nodded.

"So then I'm only *imagining* the way you go all soft and dreamy-eyed whenever you talk to me."

"Of course," she told him, feeling herself go all soft and dreamy-eyed even as she uttered the assurance.

He straightened, placed his wineglass on the mantel, then plucked hers from her hand and set it next to his. Before she realized his intention, he took a step forward, erasing what little space had separated them. He curved one hand over her jaw, curled the other around her nape and tangled his fingers in her hair. A little jolt of electricity stung her flesh everywhere his fingers settled, skittering all the way down to her toes. Miraculously, she managed not to surrender to the tremble shaking her insides.

"And I'm imagining it," he said softly, "when your skin goes all hot wherever I touch you."

"Yes," she lied, feeling her temperature skyrocket.

"Then if I kissed you," he continued, "you probably wouldn't react at all, would you?"

Instead of answering him, Renee asked, ''Why would you want to kiss me?''

''Beats me,'' he said. ''But suddenly, that's exactly what I want to do.''

And before she could stop him—not that she necessarily wanted to stop him—Garrett dipped his head toward hers.

Eight

Even though he had come to the cabin expressly to see just how far this thing between him and Renee might go, Garrett was surprised by the outcome. Not that he had succumbed so easily to his urge to kiss her—he was frankly amazed that he'd been able to wait *this* long to pull her into his arms. Nor was he surprised that she melted so willingly into his kiss—there had been an unmistakable hunger in Renee's eyes the moment she'd opened the front door.

No, what surprised Garrett was that she tasted as sweet as she did. He was surprised by the artlessness and innocence of her response. And he was surprised at the depth of his need for her—he wanted Renee more than he'd wanted anyone, any *thing,* for a long, long time.

And here she was, his for the taking. At least until next week. Then she would belong to someone else.

The reminder made Garrett pull his mouth away from hers for a moment to search her face for an answer to a question he had yet to pose. But all he saw in her expression was desire—rampant, fluid, unstoppable. Just like his own. So he dipped his head to hers again and filled her mouth with his tongue, to taste her, to possess her, as deeply as his need commanded him to.

Renee moaned in response to his invasion, splaying her hands over his chest, urging them higher to grip his shoulders tight. For a moment, Garrett thought she was trying to push him away, and instinctively, because he didn't want to let her go just yet, he clung to her even more tightly. Then he realized she was trying to pull him closer. So he roped his arms around her waist and urged her body to meet his.

He wasn't sure how long they remained so entwined, battling for control of the kiss—perhaps seconds, perhaps centuries. But around him, everything seemed to go still. The night was silent—only the hiss and crackle of the fire serenaded them, mingling with their combined, and ragged, breathing. Darkness enveloped them, eased only by the riotous dance of the flames. And Renee surrounded him—her heat, her softness, her scent—threatening to consume him whole.

Every sense he possessed was honed in on her—the way she tasted, felt, smelled, sounded—and it was the totality of his response that finally overcame him. More. Garrett wanted more. So, without questioning his motives or actions, more was what he took. Slowly, he moved his hands over the warm expanse of her back, then lower, to the curve of her waist and the flare of her hips. In response to his exploration, Renee murmured encouraging, incoherent sounds and pushed herself closer still. Her body seemed to come alive everywhere his fingers wandered, and she tasted…oh, she tasted so good.

So Garrett continued his seduction, skimming his hands lower still, until he encountered the taut curves of her bottom. Unable to help himself, he palmed the twin swells possessively before curling his fingers down even more, beneath the lower slopes. Then he pushed her forward, pulling her off the floor and against the quickly ripening evidence of his desire, rubbing the hard length of himself languidly against her.

Renee sucked in a shocked breath at the action, tightening

her fingers in his hair, nipping his lower lip lightly with her teeth. But when he feared she would push him away, she hooked her legs around his waist and clenched them tight.

Garrett growled out loud at her capitulation, dropping his mouth to the slender column of her throat, covering the distance to the sofa in a few easy, desperate strides. He bent forward and lay her atop the cushions, then followed her down, insinuating himself between her thighs in much the same way he had that afternoon. Renee again hooked her legs over his and roped her arms around his waist, searching his face in the darkness for something Garrett couldn't quite identify. So instead of pondering her expression, he dipped his head to hers and covered her mouth with his.

She tasted of passion and promise, of desire and dreams. Her body melted into his as if the two of them were two pieces separated eons ago that had finally been rejoined. At the very edge of his brain, he registered her fingers dancing along the bare flesh of his back, and in response, he moved one of his hands to the hem of her shirt. Deftly, he scooted the fabric up along her torso until he'd bared her breasts and filled his hand with the luscious prize of one. So soft. So ripe. So lush. He couldn't resist dipping his head lower still for a taste....

Renee cried out when he skittered the tip of his tongue across one taut nipple, arching her body into his as her fingers dug into his back. She was so sensitive to his touch, reacted as if she'd never experienced the simple caress of a man's mouth on her flesh. Garrett pushed the thought aside and tasted her deeply, drawing the tight little bud into his mouth for a more thorough feast. Over and over he lapped at her, sucking her deeper with every pull. And Renee lay still beneath him, as if she feared movement might put an end to his ministrations.

So Garrett took his time enjoying her, nibbling the lower curve of her ample bosom, drawing languid circles with his tongue, covering her other breast with his hand, toying with the pebbled peak. Eventually, though, Renee grew restless, writhing beneath him as if demanding the same attention for other parts of her. So, although he continued to suckle thirstily at her breast, he scooted his hand lower, easily untying the drawstring at her waist before tucking his hand beneath.

Without hesitation, he palmed the heated flesh of her belly, then deftly moved his fingers under her panties to the heart of her. Again, Renee went absolutely still at the contact, groaning incoherently as he plowed the damp folds of skin, teased the stiff bud he encountered amid them and easily penetrated her with one long finger as deeply as he could go.

Tight. Oh, she was so tight. And hot. And wet. He withdrew his finger to rub a lazy circle around her, then drove it deeply inside. He felt her shudder around his taut digit and knew she was about to come undone. Before he could say a word, though, a tremor shook her, and as she cried out in utter ecstasy, wave after wave of heat flowed over his hand. Quickly, Garrett moved to cover her mouth with his again, capturing her cries, one after another, echoing them right back at her again.

After a moment, Renee went utterly still. Her heart thundered against his, and his body burned everywhere she touched him, from his chest to his fingers to his thighs. But for a long moment, neither of them moved, neither of them spoke, neither of them seemed to breathe.

Garrett thought she would take him by the hand and lead him to her bed, to fulfill every fantasy he'd ever had. But that moment shattered when, with a single, chaste kiss, Renee struggled out of his embrace and began to rearrange her clothing. She rose quickly from the couch, and Garrett moved aside to let her do it, then hastily moved a few steps away. And then, evidently unable to even look at him, she spun to face the darkness instead.

And although she clearly didn't want him to follow her, Garrett crossed to where she stood, cupping a hand over her shoulder to urge her around. He curved the fingers of one hand over her jaw and curled the others around her nape, then he dipped his forehead to rest it against her own.

She reached up to circle her fingers around his wrists, as if she would push his hands away. But instead of doing so, she only held on tight and said, very softly, "That...that shouldn't have happened."

She was right, of course. Garrett knew she was. But he suspected the reasons for her conclusion were completely different from his. As far as he was concerned, their soul-scrambling embrace shouldn't have happened because it had made him feel and remember things he had expressly forbidden himself to feel or remember. Still, he wanted to hear her take on the matter.

"Why not?" he asked, amazed that he could keep his voice level when there were so many emotions tearing him up inside.

And damn his emotions for that. How dare they betray him at a time like this—making him *feel* things, for God's sake—ruining what might have been an otherwise very enjoyable physical reaction. But what had begun for Garrett as idle curiosity about an attractive young woman had quickly turned into a hunger for her that he couldn't quite control. And it wasn't just a physical hunger, either, dammit. No, the way he craved Renee burned much farther inside him than skin deep.

"You know why," she said, stirring him from his troubling thoughts.

Although he did know why, and he had no desire for her to put voice to the words, he said softly, "Remind me."

"Because I'm getting married in less than a week," she told him, sounding in no way certain about such a thing.

Even so, a great fist grabbed his heart and squeezed tight. He did his best to ignore the sensation. "Are you?" he asked. "Are you really?"

Renee pulled back, but she didn't release him, and her gaze never faltered from his. "Yes," she said. "I am. Unless you can give me one reason, one very good reason, that I shouldn't."

Her eyes were pleading, her lips thinned into a desperate line. She seemed to be saying, *Tell me not to marry Lyle. Tell me there's a chance for something to happen between the two of us, and I'll call off the wedding right now. Tell me that you care for me, that you want something more.*

But Garrett couldn't quite bring himself to do that. Because although he did indeed care for Renee, he wasn't sure it was enough. He wasn't sure he cared for her in the way a man should care for a woman he intended to keep close forever. Sure, he wanted her. Hell, he hungered for her. And yes, he needed her, too. For the moment, at least. But he simply could not, would not mislead her into thinking there was a chance for something more. Because he just didn't know if there *was* a chance for something more.

He wasn't sure what made him ask, but he heard himself say, "Do you love Lyle Norton?"

She swallowed hard, then slowly shook her head. Her gaze never faltered from his as she replied quietly, "No. I don't."

A wave of heat splashed his insides at her confession, but he ignored it. "Then why are you marrying him?"

She hesitated before saying, "I don't have much choice."

"Why not? Are you pregnant?"

He wasn't sure, but he thought she almost smiled at that. "No. I'm not pregnant."

"Then why?"

"He… I…" She sighed fitfully. "It's kind of complicated," she finally said.

"Just answer me one question," he said. "Honestly."

"All right."

"Is it because of his money?"

A shutter fell over her features at his question, and something cold and heavy replaced the heat in his belly. "Why do you ask that?" she said.

"Just answer the question. Are you marrying Lyle Norton for his money?"

Another tense moment passed before she told him, "Not the way you think."

"Meaning that you *are* marrying him for his money," Garrett said, the words tasting bitter on his tongue, even though he told himself he should have suspected all along it was the truth.

You dumb sap, he berated himself. *Didn't you learn your lesson the first time around?*

"It's not the way you think," she repeated emphatically. "Garrett, there's more to it than what you're—"

He jerked one hand free of the delicate fingers encircling his wrist and held it up to stop whatever lame explanation she had been about to give. "Don't." He cut her off. "Don't even bother."

"But—"

"No, Renee," he interjected. "You've told me everything I need to know."

And it was nothing he hadn't already guessed. Renee Riley was exactly the kind of woman Garrett had feared she was, exactly the kind of woman he had promised himself he would avoid. A woman who selected her suitors based on their bottom lines instead of their potential for growth.

"Well, then, Renee, I can't give you a good reason you should stop your wedding," he said. "Unless maybe it's because your loyalties don't seem to be lying exactly where they should."

A slash of pain shot through her eyes, and he almost—almost—regretted his words. Then she released his other wrist and took a step away, turning her back on him. And, thankfully, he couldn't know for sure what she was thinking. Even so, something inside Garrett screamed for him to go after her, to take her in his arms and promise her anything—*anything*—if she would only touch him again, even for a moment. But somehow, he managed to stay rooted where he was.

"My loyalties are just fine, thanks," she said. "I know exactly what I need to do. Which is why what happened tonight—with you and me, I mean—can't and won't happen again."

"Your loyalties are fine, huh?"

She nodded.

"You still intend to marry Lyle."

"Yes."

In spite of all his convictions that he had nothing to offer Renee, the realization that she would still be marrying Lyle shook Garrett to his very core. Who cared if she married Lyle? he asked himself. Garrett knew enough about her fiancé to consider the man plastic, greedy and superficial. Hell, in spite of what he'd just told her, Lyle and Renee deserved each other. There was absolutely no reason for him to feel so cheated by her insistence on marrying the guy.

But that was exactly how Garrett felt. Cheated. Abandoned. He told himself to leave now, while he still possessed some semblance of sanity. But instead, he stood rooted in place with his hands hooked on his hips. "Renee, turn around," he commanded before he could stop himself.

To his amazement, she obeyed him. And as she stood there watching him, waiting, all he could do was note how her hair was still tousled from his hands, how her lips were red and swollen from his kisses. He recalled the way her mouth had warred with his over possession of their kiss, remembered how soft and eager she'd been beneath his fingertips.

"Just tell me this," he said gruffly, wondering what devil made him demand what he was about to demand. "What happened here tonight…between you and me…how does it stack up with what goes on between you and your fiancé?"

Her expression turned almost desperate. She shook her head, hard. "Oh, Garrett, don't ask me that, please. Just drop it and forget it ever happened."

"I want to know."

"It's none of your business," she told him.

"I think what happened here tonight makes it my business," he countered.

He didn't think she would answer him, so long did she stand there staring at him. But, evidently realizing he had no intention of backing down, she finally nodded resolutely and dragged a restive hand through her dark hair. "Fine. If you must know, what happened here tonight didn't even come close to what I have with Lyle."

He tried not to flinch when she said her fiancé's name, but it lingered in the air between them. He stood motionless, waiting for her to continue.

"But this thing between you and me," she said, spurred by his silence, "it's based on simple animal attraction, nothing more. That's why it doesn't even bear comparison with what I have with Lyle. With him, it goes beyond physical."

A single muscle twitched in Garrett's jaw before he said, "Yeah, with him you have that nice financial aspect that makes things real comfortable, right?"

She glared at him. "With him, I have something more important than just animal attraction."

He glared right back. "What could possibly be more important than animal attraction?"

Renee expelled a soft sound of disbelief. "It's all a game to you, isn't it, Garrett? Everything that happened tonight…it was no big deal, nothing out of the ordinary for you."

"You got that right," he muttered. He told himself it was the truth, that Renee Riley *wasn't* any big deal, *wasn't* anything out of the ordinary and was certainly no different from any other woman in the world. But he hated having to lie to himself that way.

She nodded disconsolately. "Yeah, well, I need something a little more than animal attraction. Whatever there is between the two of us…it's not enough."

His eyebrows shot up in disbelief. "Not enough?" he echoed. "Sugar, if I'd had a few more minutes, I could have given you more than enough. Certainly more than you could handle."

Her eyes widened at his implication, heat flooding her face. "Garrett, please," she said softly, breathlessly. "Just go."

"You think you can just forget about what happened here tonight?"

"I don't know," she said, a bit less vehemently, some of the fight leaving her. "But I have a lifetime—*with someone else*," she clarified adamantly, "to try and forget it, don't I?"

Garrett nodded, but the gesture felt brittle—hell, his whole body and soul felt brittle—and he turned away. As he made his way toward the front door, he noticed the picnic basket on the table, crossed to it and withdrew another bottle of wine he'd packed inside. But instead of taking it with him, he set it, too, on the coffee table.

"Never mind," he said as he headed for the front door. "I've got a feeling I'm going to need something a lot stronger than that tonight."

Not surprisingly, he slammed the door on the way out.

Nine

The following afternoon, when Renee should have been packing her bags and planning her escape to Minneapolis, she
leaned against the kitchen counter sipping a cup of raspberry
tea, staring out the window instead. She should go home to
Minneapolis, she told herself. Go back to the wedding planning, the trousseau shopping, the last-minute detailing. Return
to the life that lay ahead of her for the rest of her days. Her
father was expecting her home by tomorrow. She might as
well pack it in today.

Instead, she sipped tea and stared out the window. Because
she couldn't go home. Not yet. Not with Garrett thinking the
things about her that he was thinking. Not until she figured
out just what on earth had happened between the two of them
the night before. And not as long as there was even the tiniest,
most infinitesimal part of her that was still hoping that
maybe—just maybe—something good and true might come
out of everything that had passed between them.

What happened last night, a traitorous voice inside her said in response, *is that you made a complete fool of yourself. And anything that's passed between you and Garrett has been nothing but a farce. It's over. Deal with it. He'll never come around.*

Renee squeezed her eyes shut tight to deny the voice, replaying the evening scene by scene, word by word, touch by touch. But in spite of her effort, she was forced to admit that she had indeed behaved foolishly. She'd let herself be overpowered by a strong hormonal feeling and had reacted in a way she never would have imagined herself capable of reacting. She had lost control, had succumbed to her desires and needs, instead of considering first the repercussions of her actions.

She had let herself feel instead of think. And, where Garrett Fortune was concerned, she really should have known better. Even if what he had made her feel had been wonderful beyond words. Even if it had been utterly unlike anything she had ever felt before. Even if it was something she would doubtless never feel again with anyone else.

This was pointless, she thought, opening her eyes. Garrett wasn't the kind of man to understand anything about duty, obligation and responsibility. Not the kind that she felt, anyway. And he certainly wasn't the kind of man to understand that there was more to falling in love than physical fulfillment.

Love, she thought. Surely it wasn't that. Not now. Not with him.

Although Renee would be the first to admit that she was governed more by her emotions than by her thought processes, she still took pride in the fact that she seldom made mistakes. Yes, she acted on instinct much of the time, but generally her instincts were very good. Even where her impending marriage to Lyle was concerned, she had acted on impulse more than thought. True, she had given more than a little consideration to Lyle's proposal—it had, after all, been a life-changing move. But ultimately, her decision to marry him had come impulsively, from the heart. Because in her heart, Renee knew she should do whatever she had to do to help her father out.

So usually she didn't worry about following her heart. Because in the past, her heart had never really steered her wrong.

With Garrett, however...

She sighed heavily. With him, her heart was in a tumult, and her brain was in an uproar. Suddenly, nothing made sense. Her instincts commanded her to try to make sense of, to pursue, what was happening between the two of them, while her brain assured her there couldn't possibly be any future in it. Her heart said, "Go." Her brain said, "Stop." And all Renee could do was stand there in the middle of the intersection, paralyzed by indecision.

She chuckled morosely. She was that clichéd image of a deer frozen in the headlights of an oncoming vehicle. But in this case, the vehicle was a big ol' tractor trailer, one that was hurtling down the highway with dangerous velocity, fueled by an unstoppable desire. That was Garrett. Ramming speed. She only wished she were constructed of materials strong enough to stop his headlong rush into disaster.

He'd said flat out, the first night she'd met him, that he didn't believe in marriage, had more than hinted at the fact that he'd been burned once and didn't intend to let it happen again. And after what Kelly had told her about Garrett's ex-wife, Renee supposed she couldn't quite blame him for being reluctant to open himself up again. To find out someone had only married you because you had money, then to have her find love with another man...

She couldn't imagine what it would feel like to be betrayed by someone you cared for. Oh, wait. Yes, she could. Because if it was anything like what Garrett had made her feel last night...

She sighed again, staring blindly at the kitchen. But all she could see was the way Garrett had looked at her just before he kissed her—so handsome, so sexy, so needful. All she could feel was that brief, explosive combustion of sensation that had rocked her when he'd touched her so intimately, so insistently, oh, so expertly. All she could recall was the exquisite *rightness* of her senses whenever he was around.

It helped not at all to remind herself that he was a potent specimen of manhood and that *any* woman would get drunk on the testosterone he exuded. Nor did it help to remind herself that there had probably been dozens of women who had fallen into his snare before her and that there would surely be dozens after her.

Because instead of diminishing him and making him less appealing, somehow such realizations only made Garrett seem that much more vulnerable to her. As if he were searching for something he hadn't been able to find. As if he feared he might never find it, no matter how hard he looked. And she wished there was some way she could make him see what was right there in front of his face, waiting for him.

Confused and irritated that she still couldn't quite make sense of what was happening between the two of them, Renee pushed thoughts of Garrett away. Instead, she forced herself to think of Lyle, to remember her impending—yes, impending—wedding. She didn't bother to correct her semantics anymore. What was the point? If she thought she had been haunted by Garrett before, she knew she was in for a totally new kind of torture.

Because before, she had simply been recalling a couple of innocent little kisses, kisses that had barely hinted at the passion that lay beneath the surface. Now she knew the depth of that passion. And not a day would go by for the rest of her life when she wouldn't recall the way he had filled her, the way he had consumed her. The way he had covered her derriere with his hands and had tried to pull her body into his. Or, perhaps, push his body into hers. Either way, her instincts had commanded her to join with him in the most ancient, most elemental way.

Her pulse quickened at the reminder, stirring in her a need for something she couldn't quite identify. Sure, she'd read about sex often enough, and she had plenty of friends who could describe in lurid detail exactly which body parts went where. But Renee had had no idea what kind of *feelings* might be involved in such an act.

Not until last night. Last night, she'd tasted passion—real, down-to-the-soul passion. She knew hunger. She knew need. She knew longing as she'd never known it before. As reluctant as she was to admit it, she was beginning to wonder if she even knew love. Thanks to Garrett, she did have some vague idea of what it would take to assuage those mysterious yearnings—both physical and emotional—that had plagued her for so many years.

And thanks to Garrett, she would spend the rest of her life wanting and needing without receiving fulfillment. Because although she would be married to another man, sharing his life, sharing his bed, she would always, always be thinking about Garrett. And she would always, always be wondering what it might have been like between the two of them if only they had made love, even once.

Unless…

Renee shoved the thought away before allowing it to fully form. No. She couldn't do that. She *wouldn't* do that. Not only would it be wrong to make love with Garrett, even once— damn, she had *tried* not to let the thought fully form, but there it was anyway—it would be self-destructive. She was an engaged woman. She had committed herself to someone else. Even if she didn't love Lyle, giving herself to Garrett—even once—would be a moral and ethical violation of what she knew was the Right Thing to do. And giving herself to Garrett—even once—would only make matters worse than they already were.

Yes, she would find some small measure of satisfaction in making love with him. Yes, the memories of even one time with him would carry her through the rest of her life with some small measure of happiness. But she would find heartache, too, in no small measure, because deep down, she knew that one time with Garrett would never, ever be enough. And that constant craving was something Renee simply did not need to carry with her throughout her life.

Still…

No, she told herself again. It would be wrong. She was

engaged to someone else. As if she needed a physical reminder, she lifted her left hand toward the window, turning it first one way, then another, marveling at the dazzling splashes of color the diamond on her finger afforded her.

As beautiful as the gem was, however, Renee only felt sick looking at it. Before she realized what she intended to do, she had set down her tea and was wiggling the ring from her finger. Without a glance, without a thought, she set it on the kitchen counter. She only wished she could leave it there without a care, as well.

Still, once she was free of the ring, she felt as if she'd unloaded a massive weight. And suddenly, thoughts of making love with Garrett began to blossom in her brain once more. And although she tried to tell herself again how wrong it would be to submit to the idea, she couldn't quite rouse the conviction she knew would be necessary to battle it. Namely, she simply repeated to herself one more time that it would be *wrong*.

But wouldn't it be more *wrong to spend the rest of your life in a loveless marriage, without ever knowing what it was like to unite with someone you* do *love?*

Renee closed her eyes and tried to ignore the treacherous voice inside her. She wasn't positive she loved Garrett. Not really. But the voice was nothing if not insistent.

Wouldn't it be more *wrong not to at least* try *to discover if there was a chance for something lasting between you and Garrett? Wouldn't it be* more *wrong to turn your back on what might be your one chance in life to find happiness?*

But what about her father? What about Riley Communications? And, hey, while she was on the subject, what about Lyle, to whom she had already promised herself?

What about him? the voice asked.

Renee sighed heavily. What about herself? she finally asked herself. What about what *she* wanted? What about her *own* happiness? If she must surrender herself to Lyle Norton for the sake of her family, then why would it be so wrong to give herself one time with Garrett? Forget responsibility for a moment, she commanded herself. What about romance? What about love? A woman *should* be in love with her first lover. She just should. And whatever she felt for Garrett… It was as close to love as Renee had ever come.

She spared a final glance at the engagement ring on the kitchen counter and told herself again that she should just pack up her things and go home—*today*. Right now. Then she thought about Garrett. She thought about Lyle. She thought about what lay ahead *for the rest of her life*.

And, somehow, Renee knew she wouldn't be going home today.

"Sandra's dead?" Garrett's fingers tightened on the telephone receiver as he tucked it between his ear and shoulder. He dropped into the chair behind his desk and stared blindly into the office of the Final Destination. "You waited until halfway through our conversation to tell me Sandra's dead? How did she die? When?"

From the other end of the line, his younger brother, Jack, sighed heavily. "I was trying to work up to it," he said. "It's not the kind of thing you just want to launch into right off the bat. But she and her fiancé were killed in a car accident last night. I don't have all the details yet, but I needed to talk to someone about it."

"Well, yeah, I guess so. She was your wife, after all."

"Ex-wife."

Garrett nodded, then realized the gesture would be totally lost on his brother. "Still…for a while there, she was a big part of your life."

Another long sigh. "Not to mention the mother of my child."

Lilly. Garrett groaned. In the shock of Jack's announcement, he had forgotten all about his little niece. "Yeah, that, too."

Jack had married Sandra Alexander right around the time Garrett had started having problems in his own marriage. At the time, he'd tried to warn his little brother about his bride, had seen in Sandra so many of the things he'd discovered in

Marianne. In many ways, Sandra had been an even bigger fortune hunter than Garrett's wife. But Jack had insisted what the two of them felt was the real thing. It wasn't based on monetary gain.

And for a while, Garrett had thought maybe he had been mistaken, because not long after Jack and Sandra married, she became pregnant. Briefly, it looked as if everything would be perfect between the two. But, as happens in life, that didn't last long. Soon after Lilly's birth, Jack and Sandra divorced.

It had torn Jack up to see Lilly go to live with her mother, and he'd done everything within his power to spend as much time with his daughter as possible. At three years old, Lilly Fortune was the only female on the planet who could turn Garrett inside out and upside down. Although he didn't see much of his niece, on those occasions when he did, the little girl went straight to a warm, fuzzy spot inside him that no self-respecting man would admit he possessed.

Which of course was nothing compared to what Jack felt for her. And now, with her mother dead…

Garrett bolted upright in his chair and switched the phone to his other ear. "What about Lilly?" he asked. "What will happen to her with Sandra gone?"

"She'll live with me now."

Boy, if ever there was a more complicated, more weighted sentence than that little five-word announcement, Garrett didn't know what it was. Naturally, it made sense that Lilly would go to live with her father now that her mother was dead. Even if Jack was in no way equipped to care for a three-year-old girl by himself.

"I'm expecting to get full custody of her," his brother continued before Garrett could say a word. "I've petitioned the court, and there's no reason to think they'll turn me down. I am Lilly's father, after all, in spite of Sandra's efforts to push me out of the picture."

There was a trace of bitterness in his voice, indicating there was still some leftover animosity where his feelings for Sandra were concerned. Then again, Garrett could hardly blame him.

He knew exactly what it felt like to be married to and divorced from the likes of Sandra Fortune. And although he'd wanted kids with Marianne before things went sour, Garrett was thankful the two of them *hadn't* procreated. The last thing he needed was something to tie him to Marianne.

Still, that Lilly was a real sweetheart.

"Just how are you going to manage things once she arrives?" Garrett asked, trying to phrase the question as delicately as he could.

"What do you mean?"

"I mean, little brother, you have no idea what goes into the care and feeding of a child that age. Hell, of any age. And then there's that pesky job of yours—vice presidents of multinational, multimillion-dollar corporations don't tend to have a lot of spare time on their hands. Who's going to watch Lilly when you're not around?"

"Look, I know," Jack said, his voice touched with exasperation. "I've already thought about that. I know my job is going to prevent me from being with her as much as I want to. And even if it didn't, I really don't know Lilly all that well, despite the fact that she's my daughter. So I guess what I'm going to have to do is hire a nanny for her."

Garrett thought for a moment. "Why don't you ask Amanda to give you a hand?"

"Amanda?" Jack asked, confusion coloring the question. "You mean my assistant, Amanda Corbain?"

Garrett made a wry face, even though his brother wouldn't see it. "Well, hell, Jack. I know you're Mr. Man-About-Town and all, but just how many Amandas do you know?"

A pause from the other end told Garrett his brother was making a mental tally.

"Yes, I meant Amanda Corbain, your assistant," he interjected dryly, to save Jack the trouble. And because his brother had a tendency to miss the obvious, he added, "You remember her, don't you? Nice, silky fall of light brown hair that makes a man want to run his fingers through it? Puppy-dog brown eyes that just lap you right up? She's a sweet-looking thing, Amanda is. I don't know how you could need reminding.''

''*Amanda?*'' Jack asked incredulously. ''You're talking about *my* Amanda?''

Well, Garrett wasn't too sure Amanda Corbain would go along with being labeled *Jack's* Amanda, but... Actually, though, on second thought, she had always gotten kind of a soft, dreamy look in her eyes whenever Jack was around. Hmm...

''Yes, your Amanda,'' Garrett said. ''She's a sweetheart. She'd be great with kids and would probably be thrilled to help you out.''

''I don't know, Garrett....''

''In the meantime, keep me informed of all the developments, will you? And if I can help out with anything, you let me know. Call me when you know the details for the funeral, too. I'll be there for you, Jack.''

''Thanks.''

The two brothers chatted and reminisced for a little while longer, then, with a strange feeling of melancholy, Garrett hung up the phone. For long moments, he sat at his desk, fingers steepled before his mouth, wondering about the emotions wheeling inside him. Sandra dead. That in itself was troubling. But little Lilly being left without a mother. And Jack, through a capricious whim of fate, becoming a full-time father to a daughter he scarcely knew.

Renee Riley coming apart in his hands last night...

Garrett grimaced. He couldn't think about anything without having Renee interrupt his thoughts. He shoved aside the memories of the previous evening that had been winding through his head since he awoke that morning, then pushed himself away from his desk. He stood, arcing his gaze around the room that had always served to comfort him.

Like Kate's cabin—and the rest of the main house—it was a symphony of honey-colored pine left natural, with windows spanning one wall that flooded the room with the buttery golden light of early evening. Pine beams crisscrossed the ceiling, and the pine floor was decorated with a scattering of rag rugs and rough-hewn furnishings. But—like the rest of the main house—it was a simple, masculine retreat, totally lacking the feminine touches of Kate's cabin.

Except for one. Renee Riley.

Now, hold on just a doggone minute....

Garrett blinked quickly, as if doing so might dispel the specter of Renee lounging in the doorway of his office. But instead of dissolving into his muddled thoughts, the vision of her remained firmly intact. She wore battered blue jeans and hiking boots and an oversize sweater the same pale green color as her eyes, one that hung down to nearly her knees. Her hair was a wind-tossed rampage of curls, and her face was kissed with pink from the crisp wind that had buffeted the house all morning.

"What are you doing here?" he asked.

"I'm sorry," she told him as she took a step into the room. "I didn't mean to eavesdrop. The back door was standing wide-open, so I came in."

"The wind must have blown it open," Garrett said. "I'm not normally that inviting a person."

She smiled a little sadly. "So I've noticed." Before he could comment, she hurried on. "Then, when I heard you on the phone, I didn't want to interrupt, so I waited here by the door. It sounded like you were talking business, and I didn't think I'd be intruding on anything personal." She hesitated, then took another step toward him. "But it was personal, wasn't it?"

He nodded. Not that it was any of her business, but… "That was my brother. His ex-wife was killed in an accident last night."

Her dark brows arrowed down in concern. "Oh, I'm so sorry."

Garrett rose from his chair, circled to the front of the desk and perched there to face her. Hooking one denim-clad leg over the other in a figure four, he smoothed a nonexistent wrinkle out of his brown flannel shirt and tried not to be affected by her slow approach. "Yeah, well, it's one of those weird things," he said. "They certainly didn't love each other anymore—if they ever even loved each other to begin with— but Sandra was a big part of his life for a few years, and the two of them had a daughter."

Renee stopped dead in her tracks in the middle of the room. She lifted her hand to her mouth, and her eyes widened with genuine distress. "Oh, my God. That's what all that was about? Your niece lost her mother?"

He nodded once, grimly.

"How old is she?"

"Three."

Evidently not knowing what to say, Renee lifted her other hand to her mouth. But the look in her eyes was a silent testimony to the feelings that were winding through her. It amazed him, the depth of her sorrow for a little girl she didn't even know.

"You like kids, do you?" he asked.

She nodded, and after a moment's hesitation, dropped her hands to her sides. "Sure. Doesn't everybody?"

"Not necessarily."

"Oh."

"It's just that you seem really worried about Lilly—that's my niece—and you've never even met her. Seems kind of curious, is all."

"Not really," she said as she took another step forward. "I lost my own mother when I was barely two."

Something deep inside Garrett chilled at her revelation. The knowledge that she had suffered such a profound loss at such an early age hit him harder than he liked to admit, blindsiding him for a moment. She seemed so untouched by tragedy, so innocent of all the bad things life had to dish out. He had assumed she came from a fully intact family, one that had not a care in the world—like the Cleavers or the Nelsons or the Cunninghams. Of course, few people lived the idyllic TV life, he reminded himself. But there was still something about Renee that made him think she transcended the grim reality most people knew as life.

"Oh," he said, the small sound totally inadequate to convey what he was feeling. "I didn't know that. I'm…I'm sorry."

"Thank you," she said. "I don't remember her, didn't really get a chance to know her, but growing up without a mother wasn't easy. So I kind of know what your niece has in store. Still, it made my relationship with my father that much stronger."

"You and your dad are close?"

She smiled, the first genuine, dazzling smile he'd seen from her since her arrival. "Boy, are we. I'd do anything for him. And he'd do anything for me. We're very devoted to each other."

So maybe there was hope for Jack and Lilly yet, Garrett thought, smiling in spite of his concern.

"Jack's got a pretty demanding job, though," he said. "He won't be able to spend a lot of time with Lilly."

"Oh, my dad's the world's worst workaholic," Renee told him. "But he still managed to find time for me while I was growing up. If a man loves his children—truly loves them— he'll make time for them. And he'll be sure that little bit of time is jam-packed with love. I wouldn't worry too much about your brother and his daughter. They'll be fine."

He chuckled. "Yeah, and Mac sure has become embarrassingly sappy where little Annie is concerned. Not to mention Annie's mom," he added thoughtfully.

"I'm sorry," she said, clearly chagrined. "I really didn't mean to eavesdrop."

He shrugged it off. "That's all right. It's not like I was talking to him about going into the witness protection program or something."

No, Renee thought uncharitably, what he had been talking to his brother about was a woman named Amanda who had a nice, silky fall of light brown hair that made a man want to run his fingers through it. And puppy-dog brown eyes that just lapped you right up. A sweet-looking thing, Amanda was, Renee repeated to herself. A woman Garrett had been talking about in a warm, affectionate—a *warm, affectionate*—voice.

"Do you want me to leave?" she asked, not for his benefit, but for her own. Suddenly, coming to the main house didn't seem like such a good idea, after all. She was still struggling with her motivations, still arguing with herself over what, in fact, was the Right Thing to do.

Garrett frowned at her. "You just got here. Why would I want you to leave?"

She shrugged. "Family stuff," she replied evasively. "I thought you might want to be alone after the conversation you just had."

He shook his head, sighing philosophically. "No. I didn't really know Sandra that well, and she and my brother didn't part on the best of terms. Even if she is the mother of his child, she treated my brother badly. I'd be lying if I said I was going to mourn her for any length of time. So...why did you come here?" he asked, the segue sounding strangely easy and seamless in light of the disparate ends of the conversation.

Renee reminded herself that she was going to be honest with him and just get right to the point. Or rather *points.* There was certainly more than one thing that she wanted to make clear. Point one—that she would be leaving the Final Destination tomorrow, and she wanted to be sure there were no loose ends when she did. Point two—that Garrett totally misunderstood her reasons for marrying Lyle Norton, and could he please try to see beyond his prejudices for once. Point three—that she very much suspected she was falling in love with him and would stay with him as long as he wanted, if only he would ask her to.

But instead of telling him any of those things, she began lamely. "I, um...I thought we needed to talk."

A shutter fell over his expression at her declaration. "Talk?" he asked blandly, glancing at the floor. "About what?"

She expelled an exasperated sound at his attempt to pretend nothing had happened the night before. But she'd already decided she wasn't going to be put off. Not when she only had one day left with Garrett. Not when she only had one chance left to see if her future held something other than a loveless marriage founded on a business arrangement.

Trying not to be *too* sarcastic in response to his indifference, she said, "Gosh, Garrett, I'll give you three guesses what we need to talk about."

He looked up at that, but his expression wasn't exactly inviting. "Well, now, let me think.... Could it be the color scheme of your wedding, the one that will be taking place in less than one week?" he asked. "Your loving intended likes true blue, but you prefer the color of money instead?"

"No," she said succinctly. Then, because she wanted to maintain some civility, she added conversationally, "Actually, I rather thought antique rose and dove gray would be nice for a spring wedding."

Garrett narrowed his eyes. "Well, if it's not the color scheme, then it must be the musicians. You couldn't get the Minneapolis Chamber Orchestra to play 'Money Makes the World Go Around,' so you have to settle for Lou Campisano and his Amazing Accordion playing 'It Had To Be You,' is that it?"

She tugged her left ear, refusing to lower herself to his goading. "Actually," she said, "I had been hoping to line up the Little Brown Jug Polka Band, but they were booked solid through Oktoberfest. So we hired a harp and flute instead. Still, if we're very lucky, they might just have 'Roll Out the Barrel' in their repertoire."

He glared at her, lips flattened into a tight line. "Then there must be a problem with the caterer," he guessed. "They want to serve those little cocktail weenies instead of Chateaubriand to all those rich folks who'll be coming, and you'll just die of embarrassment if they do."

Renee eyed him levelly for a moment before replying blandly, "No. Since it's an afternoon wedding at Lyle's mother's house, we opted for the light menu. Shrimp puffs, little quiches, spinach frittata, the usual. Of course, your testosterone level being what it is, your stomach wouldn't even notice that kind of thing. Which is immaterial anyway, seeing as how, golly gee whiz, you're *not invited.*"

"As if I'd come," he countered easily. "No, thanks. One viewing of that particular ritual was more than enough for me."

This time Renee was the one to grit her teeth. "And what ritual would that be?"

"The money-grubbing opportunist snaring the rich husband ritual."

She ignored the comment and said, "Boy, you're not very good at guessing. You didn't even come close to identifying what we need to talk about."

"Then by all means, tell me what you and I would have to discuss," he told her.

"Last night," she said, silently congratulating herself for delivering the words without a trace of uncertainty or bitterness. "We need to discuss what happened last night."

A muscle twitched in his left cheek, but he showed no other sign that he cared one way or another about the subject. And his voice was perfectly at ease when he replied, "Fine. We'll discuss last night. What about it?"

"It happened, that's what," she told him. "And now we need to talk about it."

"All right," he said agreeably. "It happened. Topic settled. Case closed. What's next on the agenda?"

"There is no next on the agenda," she said. "Because the topic isn't settled and the case isn't closed. We need to talk about it."

He shrugged, throwing a hand casually to the side before dropping it into his lap. "Then talk," he decreed impatiently.

Instead of following her own indications, however, Renee eyed Garrett in thoughtful silence, trying to figure out what it was about the man that made him so appealing to her. True, he was more handsome than even Prince Charming had a right to be, and true, he claimed enough sex appeal for an entire branch of the U.S. Armed Forces.

But there were a lot of handsome, sexy men in Minneapolis, she reminded herself. Garrett was no better looking, no more intelligent, no more articulate and certainly no more charming than any other man of her acquaintance. On the contrary, when it came to the charm department, she could probably find better candidates in the reptile house at the Minneapolis Zoo. Nevertheless, there was something about him that drew her to him, fiercely, irrevocably. She just couldn't quite say what.

Then again, who could explain the machinations of love?

Because that was what she really wanted to talk about with Garrett. Love. The fact that she might be falling in love with him. And whether there was any possibility that he might someday come to love her. Because if he thought there was even the teensiest little chance that he might grow to love her, then Renee would call off her wedding to Lyle in a heartbeat and explore whatever this thing was between them. Her father would understand, she told herself. Her lifelong happiness was at stake, after all.

Just tell him, she commanded herself. Tell him that she might finally be falling in love. When she had least expected it. Just in time for her wedding. To someone else.

"Renee?"

Hearing her name spoken in that rough voice snapped her out of her reverie, and when she looked at Garrett again, it was to find him gazing at her with a mixture of boredom and concern for her mental well-being.

"Yes?" she replied halfheartedly.

"For someone who keeps saying we need to talk, you sure aren't saying very much."

She sighed heavily. "All right. I'll talk."

Then, in complete opposition to her assertion, she realized she had absolutely no idea what to say. Because she was suddenly too caught up in noticing how wonderful Garrett smelled—like a forest full of redwoods—and how erotic the sound of his voice was when he said her name in that exasperated way he had, and how thoroughly delicious he looked—better than a slice of hot cherry pie with ice cream.

That, in turn, reminded her of how he had tasted the night

before as he'd filled her mouth, and how he had felt with his big body pressing so urgently, so demandingly into her own. And all at once, she decided that actions would speak much louder than words. So she took the two final steps that would bring her body within scant inches of his. Without thinking about it, and before she lost her nerve, she cupped a hand over each of his thighs, spread his legs open and stepped inside them.

And then, as he gaped at her in surprise, she hooked her arms around his neck, tilted her head to one side and launched herself into a kiss. The kind of kiss that he would remember on cold, lonely nights as he lay in his bed alone, wondering how she was doing—*what* she was doing—with her new husband.

Evidently, she succeeded in her effort pretty well, because, after just the tiniest, most infinitesimal hesitation, Garrett looped his arms around her waist and pulled her forward. He groaned as he ground his mouth against hers and took possession of the kiss, then splayed his hands open over her back as he pulled her closer still. He hooked his calves around her thighs, spreading her legs open, moving his hands to cup her bottom. And then he surrounded her, from shoulder to knee, and Renee nearly collapsed at the heat rushing through her.

Somehow, she managed to tear her mouth away from his, and surprisingly, Garrett let her do it. For a moment, she only gazed at him, gasping for breath, begging him silently to please, *please* listen to what she had to say. But even more than that, she hoped he would hear what she *didn't* say. Because as deep as her feelings for him ran, Renee couldn't quite bring herself to speak the words aloud just yet.

"I know you think I only agreed to marry Lyle because he has money," she began softly.

He opened his mouth to comment, but she covered it loosely with her left hand.

"And in a way, you're right," she continued. "I did accept his proposal because, financially, he's..." She sighed heavily. "He's in an advantageous position," she concluded lamely.

"Renee, I—"

"Shh," she said, pressing her fingers more insistently against his lips. "Let me finish."

He nipped her fingertips lightly with his teeth, then, at her gasp of surprise, he circled her wrist with sure fingers and lifted her hand from his mouth. "All right," he said, his voice gruff, strained. "Finish. And then I have a thing or two to say myself."

"Okay," she agreed. "Fair enough."

He continued to hold her hand as she spoke, the pad of his thumb rubbing lazy circles on the inside of her wrist. But his gaze never faltered from hers, and the grim line of his mouth never softened. Ignoring the rapid pulsing of her blood, Renee continued quietly.

"I won't go into details about why I agreed to marry Lyle," she said. "Because frankly, the details aren't important. Just know that the reason I made the choice I did was…" She faltered for a moment. "Well, it was because I didn't think I had any other choice. That doesn't make me an opportunist," she insisted when he started to speak. "In marrying Lyle, I'd be fulfilling an obligation I've had all my life. And unless I have a reason—a good, solid reason—to turn my back on that obligation, then I can't do it. Garrett, I *can't*. Not without a reason. Do you understand?"

He eyed her warily. "No," he said evenly. "I don't understand. This…" He held up her left hand, as if he were going to use it for an illustration. He opened his mouth as if he were going to argue, but when he turned his attention to her fingers, his mouth snapped shut again. "Where is it?" he asked.

She feigned confusion. "Where's what?"

He glared at her. "Your engagement ring, dammit. Where is it?"

She inhaled deeply before stammering, "I—I took it off."

"Why?"

"Because I didn't want Lyle to come between you and me when we—" She halted abruptly, catching her lower lip with her teeth, not sure she had the nerve to go through with what she'd come to do.

"When we what?" he demanded.

She expelled her breath slowly, and it came out as a shudder of uncertainty. It was now or never, she told herself. Cards on the table time. Very, very softly, she said, "When we make love."

For a long time, Garrett said nothing, only gripped her wrist loosely in his hand, his gaze penetrating, unreadable. Then, slowly, his fingers began to tighten their hold on her. He tugged once gently, pulling her closer. Then, with his free hand, he tangled his fingers in her hair.

"You're presuming an awful lot here," he told her, his voice surprisingly gentle in light of the rigid expression on his face.

"Not after last night, I'm not," she replied, splaying her free hand over his chest. Beneath her fingertips, his heart was racing as swiftly as hers, and she took comfort in the knowledge that he was no more confident of what was happening between them than she was. "If I hadn't put a stop to things last night, we would have made love. We both know that."

"But you did put a stop to it," he said softly.

Renee swallowed hard. "Yes. Last night, I did. Because I wasn't sure what was going on with us. I didn't understand."

"And tonight?"

She shook her head slowly. "Tonight I won't put a stop to it."

"Because tonight you suddenly do understand?"

She nodded once, feeling in no way confident or certain. "Yes. I do."

He made a restive sound. "Well, you're one up on me, then, sweetheart. Because I sure as hell don't understand it."

"Make love to me," she said, scarcely recognizing her own voice. "Please, Garrett. Just once. Before I—"

This time he was the one to lift a hand to her mouth, halting her words before she could voice them. For a long moment, he gazed at her in silence. Then he lowered his head to hers and brushed his thumb once, twice, three times across her lower lip before replacing his hand with his mouth.

It was quite an extraordinary kiss, unlike any of the others the two of them had shared. Where before had been fever, need and demand, this time there was uncertainty, tentativeness and solicitude.

And then slowly, very slowly, he pulled his head back, opening his eyes to meet her gaze head on. And what Renee saw in his eyes nearly stopped her heart. Raw hunger. Total desire. And maybe, just maybe…

Softly, he said, "You want me to make love to you, Renee, honey? Well, all right. We'll make love." He set her at arm's length and eased himself off the desk. As he did, his lips curled into something of a smile, but there was no happiness, no satisfaction, no gentleness in the gesture. His voice was gritty as he promised, "In fact, sweetheart, I'll do everything in my power to make damned sure you remember this night all through your entire married life."

And without awaiting a response, he wove his fingers through hers and tugged her along behind him toward the stairs.

Ten

Garrett's bedroom was on the darker side of the house, but was still warmed by the soft rays of the setting sun. As Renee entered behind him, she stole a swift survey of her surroundings, noting as she had elsewhere in the main house the bare pine walls, the curtainless windows, the scattering of rugs and furnishings that took their cue from the great outdoors. What were doubtless family photographs peppered the walls here and there. The pine dresser sported little more than masculine necessities, a ladder-back chair beside it. The bed was rough-hewn and smaller than she would have expected, covered by what appeared to be a handmade quilt.

The windows were flanked outside by two tall, proud evergreens, the sky between them darkening to a soft violet and orange. A squirrel chattered at the setting sun, a couple of starlings argued over a bit of supper, and a soft breeze whispered through the trees. But otherwise, the evening was silent.

On the opposite side of the room, a fireplace spanned a good part of the wall. It was obviously well used, with wood and kindling positioned to await the strike of a match. Renee watched as Garrett crossed to do just that, taking a few moments to light a fire in place of a lamp. Then again, that was just as well, she decided. Because she wasn't sure she'd be comfortable right now in the bright, false illumination of lamplight.

Within minutes, the fire was crackling and licking at the logs, and Garrett stood and turned to face her. Renee inhaled a slow, calming breath, one that neither slowed nor calmed her senses. He was just so…so much a man, she thought. She'd always thought her first time would be with someone more like her—someone who was young, inexperienced, uncertain. Instead, her first time would be with someone who was very experienced. Very certain. Very…everything.

Ah, well, she thought. At least she would be in love with her first. Not everyone could say that.

He said nothing as he strode lazily across the room. Nothing as he lifted his hands to her shoulders. Nothing as he pulled her close to him again. But instead of crushing her to him and fastening his mouth to hers, as he had downstairs, this time Garrett only held her close and tucked her head beneath his chin. He folded his arms over her shoulders to rub his open palms slowly, casually up and down her back.

Renee closed her eyes as she circled his waist with her arms and took a moment to *feel* him surrounding her. He felt so good. So right. So very perfect in her arms.

So she nestled her head against his warm chest, filled her lungs with the masculine scent of him, listened to the ragged *thump thump thump* of his heart beneath her ear.

He would be hers for tonight, she told herself. And she would be his. For tonight. In this moment, that was the only thing that mattered.

As if she'd spoken the thought out loud, Garrett curled a finger under her chin and gently tipped her head until she was looking at him. He met her gaze inquisitively, as if he wanted to be absolutely certain this was what she wanted. In that moment, Renee knew she still had an opportunity to reconsider.

But there was no way she would reconsider. There was no way she would deny herself this one gift. She had the rest of her life to repay her father for all the sacrifices he had made along the way. But first, tonight, she would take something for herself. Her memory of this one time with Garrett would make all the others that followed with someone else bearable.

So instead of telling him no, she pushed herself on tiptoe and brushed her lips lightly against his. Immediately, he tightened his hold on her, pulling her off the floor to counter her tender kiss with a less tender one of his own. Without hesitation, he slipped his tongue into her mouth, rolling it in deep to taste all of her, spearing her again and again and again.

Renee squirmed as she sought purchase but found only Garrett. So she clung to him. Heat seeped through her body, fire through her soul, as he continued to kiss her. And he kept on kissing her as he began to move, carrying her, with her body flush along the length of his, to his bed. The subtle friction of their bodies as they went only served to inflame Renee more, and she tried to push herself even closer to him, mindless of the fact that they were already as close as they could be.

When they reached the side of the bed, Garrett continued to hold and kiss Renee as he tugged the quilt and coverings down to the foot. Then he seated himself on the edge of the mattress and settled her in his lap, curling one hand over her hip, splaying the other over her belly. She lifted her hands to frame his face, cupping her palms over his warm, rough jaws, slanting her head to gain control of the kiss.

Surprisingly, Garrett let her take the lead, and Renee plundered him at will. As she did, he shifted her body until she was straddling him, facing him, intensifying their kiss. His hands scraped along her ribs and back, up and down, forward and backward, as if he couldn't quite decide which direction held the most allure. Finally, he sent one hand north and one south, cupping a breast and her bottom at the same time.

She gasped at the intimate caresses and caught fire everywhere he touched her. Through the fabric of her sweater, he palmed her soft breast to ripeness, curving his other hand deep into the taut denim covering her fanny. Then he moved his hands in unison, simultaneously drawing lazy circles, then squeezing his plump prizes, then rubbing the pleasurable ache away before starting the cycle again.

Renee didn't know where she found the courage to do it, but she pulled back from Garrett long enough to cross her hands over her torso and scoop her sweater over her head. Garrett smiled lasciviously as he fingered the delicate lace of her brassiere, not to mention the soft skin beneath. Renee smiled just as salaciously as she went to work on the buttons of his shirt.

When she freed the last one, he released her long enough to shrug out of the garment and toss it to the floor. Greedily, she tangled her fingers in the soft, springy hair that darkened his entire torso, raking the ripples of muscle beneath. She'd never touched a man so intimately before, had never realized what a mixture of hard and soft, of rough and smooth, a man could be. So she let her hands rove freely all over him, from shoulder to shoulder, from breastbone to flat belly, absorbing every inch of him as she went.

So engrossed did she become in her exploration that she didn't realize until too late that Garrett had reached behind her to unfasten her bra. And then his warm hands were on her bare flesh, as they had been the night before. Renee gasped her joy at the sensations that quickened inside her, at the heat that warmed her and the tremors that rocked her.

"Oh," she said softly. "Oh, Garrett…"

"You are so beautiful," he told her reverently. He dipped his head to feather a half-dozen kisses across her breasts. "So sweet." He breathed against her bare flesh before filling his hands with her. "So soft. I could just sit here forever touching you. Tasting you."

As if to fulfill the promise, he lifted one breast to his lips, mouthing as much as he could of the dusky peak. Renee cried out again, cupping both hands behind his neck, driving her fingers into his hair. For long moments, Garrett consumed her, laving her, suckling her, nipping her. He palmed her shoulder blades with much affection, then gradually pulled her toward him, down to the mattress. When she lay atop him, Garrett sucked her even deeper into his mouth, splaying both hands across her bottom to push her into the cradle of his thighs.

He ripened against her immediately, then rubbed his entire body languidly along hers. Acting purely on instinct, Renee arched her body into his, then was amazed to hear him gasp in much the way she had. The realization that she held him as much in thrall as he did her heartened her, strengthened her, offered her a heady sense of power. So she arched against him again. And again. And again.

"Renee, honey," he said, tearing his mouth away from her breast, "you better cut that out if you want this to last longer than a few minutes."

Uncertain what he meant by his warning, she replied, "Just how long were you planning to make it last?"

He smiled, a smile full of wickedness and intent. Then, very low, he murmured, "All night long, baby. All night long."

Her mouth suddenly went dry, and she realized she was in way over her head with Garrett. She tried to think of some snappy comeback that would make her sound worldly and sophisticated, but all that came out was a tight little sound of near terror. Garrett must have mistaken it for something else, however, because he chuckled low and rolled until their bodies had switched positions. When she was flat on her back beneath him, he wedged a hand between them and deftly unsnapped her jeans, then lowered the zipper without ceremony.

He pinned her with his gaze as he slipped his hand inside her waistband. Renee's heart kicked up an erratic rhythm as he continued down, down, down, tucking his fingers beneath the waistband of her panties, reclaiming the dewy prize he'd won the night before. She inhaled a ragged breath as he stroked one long finger over her, then closed her eyes at the explosion of heat that rocked her.

"Don't," he commanded in a rough voice. "Open your eyes, Renee. Look at me when I touch you. I want to watch while you come undone."

She was helpless to disobey him. Opening her eyes, she tried to focus on his face. But then he moved his hand again, nudged his fingers deeper. He rubbed a gentle path to and fro, around and around, in and out, then started the rhythm all over again. And again, her eyes began to flutter closed. Immediately, she opened them, and he smiled that predatory smile. More and more intimately he touched her, deeper and deeper he penetrated her. But she never looked away. Even when the threads of her sanity began to unravel, she continued to watch the fire in his eyes burn brighter.

"You're so tight, Renee," he whispered in a rough voice unlike any she'd heard from him before. "So hot. So slick. It's going to be so good between us, sweetheart. So good."

"Oh," she said again when that tight coil of heat inside her began to grow taut. "Oh, Garrett. Oh… *Oh*… Oh, *Garrett*…"

Waves of fire shuddered through her at her climax, but still she kept her eyes open, still she watched Garrett as he watched her. And just as the last of the ripples began to subside, he removed his hand long enough to tug her jeans down around her hips.

Renee could only lay limp as he removed the rest of her clothing, then his. She was only halfway coherent when he rejoined her on the bed, sheathed in a condom. Clearly unable to prolong their intimate exploration of each other, he knelt between her legs, gripping an ankle fiercely in each hand. Then, opening her wide, he moved himself forward on his knees and thrust himself deep, *deep* inside her.

Never had Renee felt such sharp pain as she did when Garrett broke through the barrier no man had come near before. And that pain was made public when she cried out her distress. Loudly. Tears sprang to her eyes and quickly spilled over, and she fought to catch a breath that might ease the pressure inside her. But all she could do was gasp without relief, squeezing her eyes shut tight in an effort to stop the tears.

Garrett went absolutely still above her, his face, when she finally opened her eyes to look at him, contorted with utter disbelief. He didn't move, didn't alter his pose, only remained buried inside her, stretching her, initiating her, branding her for life.

"Renee?" he finally said, his voice barely a whisper. "Is there something you forgot to tell me?"

She started to close her eyes again, then opened them, staring at his face as he had hers moments ago, needing to see his expression when he heard what she said. "I wanted to be in love the first time," she told him. "I wanted it to be with someone special."

But his expression told her nothing of what he might be thinking or feeling. "But your fiancé..." he began.

She shook her head. "He and I have never... You're my first, Garrett. My only. Only you."

He continued to gaze at her without speaking, without moving. For a moment, she feared he would withdraw, would turn away and reject her. So she moved her body against his in a way she hoped would change his mind. His lips parted when she did, his pupils going darker, but still he didn't move.

"Please," she said, reaching up to cup a hand over his nape. "Please, Garrett. Don't stop. Make love to me. Please."

She realized she was close to begging, so she stopped talking and told him again with her body what she wanted. This time, Garrett was the one to close his eyes, and he started to slowly withdraw. But just as Renee opened her mouth to object, he rocketed his body forward again, burying himself inside her as far as he could go. Impulsively, she wrapped her legs around his waist, holding him in place as he pelted her over and over.

Gradually, the pain eased, to be replaced by an urgency unlike anything she'd ever experienced. Then pleasure. Wave after wave of pleasure. She moved her body in time with his until he lifted her from the bed completely and wrapped her more securely around himself. Gripping her hips in his hands, curling his fingers into the tender flesh of her fanny, he moved her against himself, pummeling her more insistently, until Renee was nearly insensate with desire. And then, just when she thought she could tolerate no more, he went rigid against her, wrapping his arms tightly around her. Immediately after he did, those familiar shudders of heat uncoiled inside her one after another.

They cried out together, completed together, climbed over the top together. Then, together, they fell to the bed, front to front, face to face.

Tenderly, Garrett stroked her cheek with his fingertips, brushed her sweat-dampened hair from her eyes, searched her face as if seeking an answer to an unspoken question. But he said nothing of what had just happened, nothing of what he was thinking or what he was feeling. With one quick kiss to her temple, he rose from the bed and left the room. Renee heard the sound of running water elsewhere in the house and realized he was tending to the aftermath of their loving. Unable to help herself, she closed her eyes.

When she opened them again, Garrett's bedroom was shadowed by the half-light of dawn. But the bed beside her was empty.

A virgin.

Damn.

How had *that* happened?

Garrett sat astride his big chestnut mare, Eloise, and watched as the first fingers of dawn reached over the eastern horizon. In the distance, against a backdrop of pale pink and lavender, green hills rose and fell in lush, smooth lines, reminding him of all the curves and valleys on Renee that he'd enjoyed the night before. He'd explored every inch of her while she lay sleeping in his bed, oblivious to his scrutiny. First with his gaze, and then, when he hadn't been able to resist, with his touch.

Lightly, so as not to awaken her, he'd run a fingertip over every dip and swell, had leaned in to inhale the musky woman scent of her, had tasted with featherlight kisses her soft skin. Once or twice she had sighed in her sleep or uttered some soft sound of surrender in response. She'd stretched her naked body out along his, then curled up next to him, doubling her fists lightly against his chest, burrowing her head beneath his chin. She'd looked so beautiful, so perfect, so right lying there in his bed beside him that Garrett hadn't wanted to think about her going anywhere else. Ever.

And as he'd lain beside her, caressing and kissing her, he'd realized that caressing and kissing wasn't enough, would never be enough. He'd found himself wanting to awaken her, to make love to her again. And again. And again. The only thing that had stopped him from rousing her had been his fear that she might not be up to more after the way he'd manhandled her that first time. That he might have hurt her—both physically and emotionally—with his carelessness, with his single-minded need for her. That she would look upon him with fear instead of the warm, wistful wantonness that had been in her eyes when she'd initially asked him to make love to her.

Well, that and the rampant terror coursing through him that a second time—or even a third or fourth—with Renee wouldn't come close to satisfying him, that he'd never, not in a million years, have enough of her.

As the sun brightened the horizon with its appearance, Garrett wondered yet again what the hell was going on. Last night, he told himself, he and Renee had enjoyed sex with each other. That was all it had been. Sex. They'd both felt a physical itch and they'd simply responded instinctively, honestly, by reaching out to each other in an effort to do something about it.

Sex, he repeated to himself adamantly. It had been nothing more than sex. And he'd had sex lots of times, with lots of women. Just because it had been Renee this time, why did that make a difference?

Because it had been a first for her, he told himself. *He* had been a first for her.

Her first, he marveled again. Then he remembered something she had said right after he'd entered her and discovered her untried state. She'd not only called him her first, but her only. And she had said that she wanted to be in love with her first.

Her first. Her only. That couldn't possibly mean what it seemed to mean. Could it?

Words, he told himself. They were just words. People said the damnedest things when they were in the throes of passion. And because last night had been Renee's first time, she couldn't possibly have been thinking about what she was saying, couldn't possibly have meant to say what she seemed to have said.

Could she?

Still, Garrett couldn't quite chase away the image of her gazing at him with those soft, hungry eyes when she'd said she wanted to be in love the first time she gave herself to a man. But Renee was an engaged woman, after all, he reminded himself brutally. The simple removal of the ring from her left hand didn't change that. An engaged woman who'd said flat out that she didn't love the man she was supposed to marry.

And a woman like Renee—so young, so inexperienced, so desperate to do the right thing—might not have any trouble convincing herself, even temporarily, that she *was* in love with Garrett.

So he knew he really shouldn't read anything into what she'd implied last night. As much as he might want to. Unless it was just that both of them were totally confused about whatever was going on between them.

It bothered him, though, to let it—to let her—go so easily. He told himself that was because he wasn't finished with her yet, because that one taste of her last night wasn't nearly enough to satisfy him. But he wondered, too, if there would ever come a time when he *had* had enough of Renee?

Then, magnanimously, he told himself that letting her go now wouldn't be fair to her, either. He hadn't made it good for her last night. A woman's first time with a man was never as good as it should be, as good as it could be. He knew he'd hurt her. He'd made her cry. Had he known it was her first time, he would have been gentler with her, more giving. He wouldn't have taken so much for himself right off the bat.

If he could make love to Renee a second time, he knew

he'd make it good for her. He'd take it slower, be sure to touch her and kiss her and taste her in all the right places. Slowly. Leisurely. Thoroughly.

The next time he made love to Renee—and he knew there would definitely be a next time, because he wasn't going to let her go anywhere until he'd made up for last night—he'd show her a side of physical pleasure she wasn't likely to enjoy again. Ever. Not with another man, anyway.

So maybe it wouldn't be out of place for Garrett to ride on back to the house for round two. It could be his wedding present to her, he told himself, congratulating himself again for being just so damned magnanimous. Make sweet, passionate, mind-numbing love to Renee for the rest of the day before she returned to Minneapolis and the man she would make her husband. Show her what she'd be missing out on for the rest of her life.

Renee deserved that much, after all, he told himself. She deserved to know what she'd be missing. He turned Eloise and urged her into a steady canter to the house. He deserved to know what he'd be missing, too.

But she wasn't at the house when Garrett rode back. The bed was still warm and rumpled and redolent of her scent, but Renee was nowhere to be found. Strange, since he'd stopped by the cabin, too, just to be sure, and hadn't found her there, either.

They must have just missed each other, he thought. But if that were the case, then they would have crossed paths. The only way from the main house to Kate's cabin was the winding little path Garrett had shown Renee her first night at the Final Destination. If he'd missed her, then it was because she had heard him coming and had deliberately hid from him.

But why would she do something like that? he asked himself. She loved him. She'd told him so.

Yeah, right.

He gazed for another moment at the bed, all tumbled and wrinkled from their loving, and he couldn't quite bring himself to make it up just yet. Instead, he jerked his sweater over his head, toed off his boots and went to work on his jeans. Although he was reluctant to take a shower, too, because he didn't want to wash away the scent of Renee that lingered on his skin, he knew he would become ripe before the day was through if he didn't.

He lifted a hand to his rough jaw. Plus, he needed a shave. A man wanted to look his best, after all, when he was paying a call on a woman he'd been responsible for deflowering only hours ago. He just hoped Renee wouldn't slam the door in his face when he arrived. He still wasn't sure of the reception he was going to receive when he went to see her. Even if what he had in mind would be a favor, she just might not see it that way at first.

Shucking his jeans and briefs, Garrett strode naked to the bathroom. He had a full day ahead of him. Even if he was planning to spend the bulk of it in bed, he might as well be prepared for it.

Renee hadn't been expecting company when she heard the knock at the cabin's front door, especially Garrett. Although she had awakened alone in his bed just before dawn, she'd thought he would be in his house somewhere—fixing coffee or taking a shower or performing some other normal morning ritual. But she'd searched high and low for him only to discover that he hadn't been anywhere, and she'd remembered that this morning wasn't normal at all. Even after she'd taken advantage of his shower—warming all over as she'd sudsed herself with his soap and his shampoo—he hadn't come back.

Which had forced her to draw the conclusion that he wanted to be some place where she wasn't. And that he was giving her plenty of time to vacate the premises before he returned. So, trying to ignore all the oddly pleasant aches in her body that hadn't been there when she'd fallen asleep, she had dressed in her clothes of the day before and found her way to the cabin.

She'd almost encountered him on her return, had heard the

sound of a horse coming toward her down the path and had known it would be Garrett. For a moment, she'd braced herself to meet him, toe-to-toe and head-to-head, had straightened, squared her shoulders and lifted her chin in preparation for the face-off. But at the last minute, she'd chickened out. Frantically, she'd searched for a place to hide and had been forced to dive behind the cover of a big bush. Garrett had passed by without seeing her, without sensing her, without caring about her.

Hey, what had she expected? She asked herself that at the cabin as she changed into a fresh pair of jeans and an oversize red-and-black plaid flannel shirt. She couldn't possibly have satisfied him the night before, couldn't possibly have offered him anything memorable. She'd been a clumsy virgin who hadn't had the first idea what to do to please a man. Why would he want to spend any more time with her than he had to?

Thinking back, she realized she *hadn't* done anything to please him. She hadn't explored all those intriguing masculine areas she had wanted to explore, hadn't kissed every warm inch of him, hadn't tasted the parts of him she'd fantasized about tasting. She had just lain there in his bed like a dead fish while he impaled her, amazed at the things he made her feel.

Not that the impaling hadn't been enjoyable, mind you. And she certainly hadn't felt like a dead fish as he'd opened her wide beneath him. On the contrary, she'd never felt more sensational, more energetic, more alive. Yes, when he'd entered her that first time, it had been painful. She'd never dreamed how much it could hurt. But that pain had been short-lived, and the feeling of utter fullness and completion that had come after it had been unlike anything she'd ever experienced.

She'd felt as if Garrett became one with her in that moment. She'd felt as if the two of them joined together that way constituted one being, one soul. She'd felt his pulse pounding in time with her own, had sensed his heat mingling with hers. And for a moment, she had been certain that the two of them were fused together as one entity, that they would never, ever part.

But they had parted. And Garrett had left. And now… She sighed heavily as she tucked a pair of socks into her tote bag—white cotton anklets, so virginal, so chaste. So utterly inappropriate. Now, Renee thought, it was her turn to leave. She'd been packing the last of her things when the knock had sounded at the front door, and as she tugged the zipper closed, the rapping echoed again, louder this time.

She didn't know too many people in Last Resort, Wyoming—or even two people, for that matter—so she was pretty confident she knew the identity of her caller even before she opened the door and saw him standing there, dressed in snug blue jeans and an oatmeal-colored sweater, freshly showered and shaved. She tried to determine what he might be thinking—what he might be feeling—but his expression was inscrutable. His eyes—those soft, brandy-colored eyes—looked tired, though. Weary.

Wistful?

No, surely that was just a trick of the late morning light. Why would a man like Garrett feel wistful about anything that had happened last night? He'd probably only come to help her carry her bags to the main house and aid her in packing the car. Anything to hurry her departure from the Final Destination.

"Hi," she said softly, gripping the side of the front door tightly in an effort to keep herself standing—her legs suddenly felt like rubber, in spite of the achiness that still plagued them.

"Hi," he replied, his voice low, soft.

Seductive? Surely not. That was doubtless just wishful thinking on her part.

He glanced past her, into the cabin, and his gaze must have lit on the two bags she'd arrived with, perched for flight on the floor behind her. "You going somewhere?" he asked.

"Home," she told him. "I have to go home today. My father is expecting me. I'm supposed to meet your aunt's pilot at the airstrip in a little over an hour."

"An hour?" he echoed, and she thought—hoped—he sounded disappointed.

"Hey, no time like the present, right?" she said, injecting a cheerfulness into her voice that was nowhere near genuine. "I got what I came here for. Rest. Relaxation. Introspection." *Sex,* she added silently. Not that that had been a priority at first.

"Yeah, but…"

"But what?" she asked. *Tell me,* she wanted to say. *Just give me one reason to stay. One reason, Garrett. That's all it would take.*

He shook his head. "I just thought maybe we could talk, that's all."

Funny, she thought, the way they'd traded places in less than twenty-four hours. Last night, it had been Renee who wanted to talk. Now, however, talking was the last thing on her mind. She wasn't sure she could bear to hear whatever Garrett had to say. Because after last night, whatever he wanted to tell her couldn't possibly be good. Could it?

"I don't know," she said. "The last time one of us wanted to talk, we ended up not doing much talking."

His eyes darkened at the reminder, though whether in anger or hunger, Renee couldn't be sure. "And is that such a bad thing?" he asked.

She shrugged, hoping the gesture looked a lot more casual then it felt. "Depends on whether you were planning to have our discussion turn out the same way it did last night."

His voice revealed nothing when he asked, "What if that's exactly my plan?"

"Then I have to go," Renee told him.

"Why?"

"Because."

"Because why?"

"I just do, okay?"

He shifted his weight from one foot to the other, hooking his hands loosely on his hips. Exasperation, she thought, not sure whether that was a good sign or not. Still, it was better than indifference, right?

"No, it's not okay," he told her. "I think we need to talk. Again."

"Why?" she demanded. "Because I didn't do it right the first time?"

He hesitated before replying very softly, "No. Because *I* didn't do it right the first time."

Gee, that sort of came out of nowhere, Renee thought. A great fist wrapped around her heart and squeezed hard at the way he was looking at her. As if he hadn't had nearly enough of her. As if he wanted—and intended to get—more.

"Wh-what do you mean?" she stammered.

Again, he hesitated before replying. "I mean that if I had known last night was your first time, Renee, it would have made a difference."

Her heart began to pound fiercely at his admission. "A difference how?" she asked.

"If you'd told me it was your first time, I would have been more careful with you. I was just so hot, so turned on, so anxious to be inside you that I didn't stop to think. I just reacted. I figured we had all night to do it all different ways, and I didn't think you'd mind if the first time was fast and furious. I thought you wanted it fast and furious, too."

Just like that, Renee became hot and anxious all over again. Hearing him speak so explicitly of what had happened the night before, she found herself wanting to sway toward him, to do it fast and furious again, right there on the floor. But before she could say a word, he continued, his voice a bit rougher than it had been before.

"If I'd known that first time was your first time, I would have gone slower with you. I would have made it better for you. More enjoyable. More memorable."

Better? Renee marveled. *More* memorable? Than *that?* Was he kidding? She couldn't imagine anything being better or more memorable than last night had been.

Then the full force of what he was telling her hit her, and

the little spark of hope that had flickered to life inside her quickly sputtered and died. Because she realized then that, yes, Garrett did want more, but not of the same thing she did. Oh, sure, she would have loved to tumble right back into bed with him and make love with him again—more than she cared to admit, under the circumstances. But not just because she wanted him physically—because she wanted him emotionally, too. Spiritually. Intellectually. Psychologically.

Totally. Irrevocably.

She had been hoping he meant something else when he'd said knowing last night was her first time would have made a difference. She'd thought perhaps he would understand the depth of her feelings for him. She had thought it might change his feelings for her, his opinion of her.

But by his own admission, the only difference it would have made would have been in his physical performance, not in the way he felt about her. Evidently, feelings hadn't entered into it at all last night. Not for Garrett, anyway. He'd just wanted to make sure they had a good time. Gosh, that was just so damned nice of him.

"Forget about it," she told him, not sure what else to say.

His eyes darkened again. "Is that what you're planning to do? Forget about it?"

She threw him a look that would leave no doubt about just how unlikely that was, but she said nothing.

"All right, if you won't answer that one, then let me ask you this. What are your plans when you get back to Minneapolis?"

She narrowed her eyes. "What do you mean?"

"I mean, what are your plans?"

This was too much, Renee thought. Here her heart was breaking into a million pieces, and Garrett was too blind to even see what was going on. She couldn't quite help her haughty tone as she told him, "Oh, gee, I don't know. I guess first I'll unpack my bags and hang up my clothes so they won't be all wrinkled. I just hate wrinkled clothes, don't you? Then I suppose I'll have a late lunch. Chicken salad maybe, or a club sandwich. Maybe I'll even order something to be delivered. After that, I'll probably do a little reading, maybe watch a little TV, that kind of thing. Then—"

"You know what I mean, Renee." He cut her off in mid-sarcasm.

She frowned. "No, I'm afraid I have no idea what you mean, Garrett."

He inhaled a deep breath and let it out slowly, his gaze never wavering from hers. "Are you still planning on getting married this week?"

She gazed at him without answering, swallowing hard against the bitterness that rose to the back of her throat. Then, very slowly, she nodded. "Of course I'm still planning to get married. Why wouldn't I be?"

It's now or never, Garrett, she thought. *Here's your chance to change my mind. Don't blow it.*

His lips thinned into a tight line. "So last night made no difference to you?"

Renee knew there was no way she could lie to him about her feelings where last night was concerned. Nor did she want to. "Last night…" she began. But she had no idea how to describe the tumult of emotion inside her. She sighed fretfully, but she couldn't quite meet his gaze as she spoke. "Last night… Last night was wonderful, Garrett. Truly. I mean, I know it wasn't wonderful for you, me being so inexperienced and all. I'm sorry I was no good. You couldn't possibly have enjoyed yourself, but—"

"Who says I didn't enjoy myself?"

She studied his face, looking for some sign that he was telling her the truth. But his expression was impassive. "You mean…you *did* enjoy yourself?" she asked.

"Hell, yes, I enjoyed myself."

Wow, it must be true what all her friends had told her, Renee thought. Evidently, bad sex really was better than no sex at all.

She pushed the thought away. "Then I guess the question, Garrett, is whether or not last night made a difference to *you.*"

His gaze narrowed. "What do you mean?"

She lifted a shoulder and let it drop. "Have your feelings changed?" she asked.

A muscle twitched in his jaw, but he offered no indication otherwise that he had heard what she said. She was about to repeat the question when he finally replied, "Feelings? What feelings?"

Her heart dropped right to the bottom of her stomach at the complete lack of emotion in his response. Well, that pretty much told Renee all she needed to know, right there. If he hadn't had any feelings for her, then they couldn't very likely have changed simply because the two of them had made love.

Had sex, a voice inside immediately corrected her. There hadn't been a bit of love involved.

"Never mind," she said softly. "It's not important. None of it is important." *Not to you, anyway.*

"So you're still planning to leave today?" he asked.

"Yes."

"Still planning to get married?"

"Yes."

"You're just going to walk away from the last few days?"

Her head snapped up at his question, and she met his gaze levelly. "Are you going to tell me that you *won't* just be walking away from them? That they actually meant something to you?"

Again, that muscle twitched in his jaw, but his expression remained unchanged. "No, I'm not going to tell you that."

"Because the last few days meant nothing to you, is that it?"

Instead of answering her, he stood still and glared at her.

"Fine," Renee said wearily, suddenly wanting to be anywhere but here.

"Fine," he echoed.

For a long moment, they stood in the doorway staring at each other in silence. Renee got the impression that there was more, much more, that Garrett wanted to tell her, but he said nothing, made no effort to speak. Finally, when the silence became more than she could tolerate, she shoved herself away from the door and retreated into the cabin to collect her bags.

"Let me help you," Garrett said from behind her.

"No, thank you," she told him. "I think you've done enough."

But he ignored the comment, striding easily past her to pick up both bags, grasping one firmly in each hand. "It's the least I can do," he said quietly as he straightened and made his way through the door. He never glanced her way once.

They made the walk to the main house, to Renee's rented car, in silence. Garrett maintained a steady, rapid pace, and Renee didn't bother to try to keep up with him. Eventually, he was too far ahead of her to hear her, had she wanted to say something else to him. And although there were indeed plenty of things she would have liked to tell him, she supposed it was just as well that he was beyond reach.

Because she probably would have only made a fool of herself. Again. This way, Garrett might at least remember her as someone he'd enjoyed—even if only physically—however briefly, however superficially. He wouldn't recall her as a lovesick virgin who'd lost herself to him body, heart and soul. He wouldn't remember her down on her knees begging him to please, please love her the way she loved him.

By the time she rounded the main house to the driveway, Garrett had placed her bags in the back seat and disappeared. So that was it, she thought. He wasn't even going to say goodbye. With one final glance around the Final Destination, Renee made her way across the yard and into the car. It started easily, and she threw it into reverse and backed in an arc to face the vehicle in the other direction.

But as she urged the accelerator slowly to the floor, she couldn't resist one final glance in her rearview mirror. And when she did, she saw Garrett standing at the front window, gazing at her car as she pulled away. Without looking back, her heart pounding rapidly, she steered the car with her left hand and lifted her right in farewell. Surprisingly, Garrett lifted his hand in response.

Then, with a crunch of gravel and a heavy sigh, Renee drove slowly away. And she wondered if there would ever come a time in her life when she would stop wishing that the Final Destination had been exactly that—her final destination.

Eleven

The Saturday morning in April that Renee had set aside for her wedding dawned bright and beautiful with promise. She awoke with a sense of duty, a sense of purpose. She donned her white teddy and white stockings, slipped the dress of billowing white lace and pearls and roses over her head, stepped into her little white satin slippers. She pushed her dark curls atop her head with combs, crowned them with her long white veil and finished with her mother's pearl necklace and drop earrings. And all the while she assured herself over and over again that what she was doing was the Right Thing.

Funny, though, how it all felt totally, inconceivably wrong. Except for the times when she found herself thinking of Garrett Fortune. Had she been dressing in her wedding finery to marry *him*... Well, that would have felt like the Right Thing to do.

As Renee stood in front of the cheval mirror in her bedroom, gazing at the stranger reflected at her, a wave of nausea rolled through her, and she realized what a farce she was playing. What a farce she'd been playing for months.

She couldn't kid herself any longer. There was no way on earth she could go through with this wedding. She didn't love Lyle. She would never love Lyle. And Lyle didn't love her. She would never be happy trapped in a marriage of convenience, and if she was miserable, Lyle would be, too. It wasn't fair to marry him when she was in love with another man. And it wasn't fair to Renee, either.

Because she definitely was in love with Garrett. As much as she'd tried to convince herself that she had only been infatuated with him, not in love, she knew better. And she knew, too, that she'd been kidding herself when she'd thought making love with Garrett once would make the rest of her life with Lyle bearable.

She had no life with Lyle. She knew that now. Making love with Garrett had simply served to make her see how life without him would be completely unbearable. Even if he didn't love her, even if the two of them had no future together, even if she never saw him again, she would never be able to forget him.

She would never be able to stop loving him.

But how was she going to tell Lyle that she couldn't marry him? How could she abandon him, leave him at the alter? He deserved better than some clichéd end to their relationship, however dubious that relationship had been. She glanced at the clock on her dresser—one o'clock. The wedding was only two hours away. Lyle and his family were expecting her at their house in less than an hour. Guests would be arriving soon. How was Renee going to break the news to all of them?

Be honest, she told herself. *For once in your life, just tell the truth. To everyone.*

A soft rap at her bedroom door scattered her troubled thoughts, and she turned toward the summons as her father called out.

"Renee, honey?" he asked. "Can I come in?"

"Sure, Daddy."

He pushed the door open and entered, but he didn't look happy. How odd, she thought. Her father had fairly been dancing a jig since her return from Wyoming, had divided his time between telling Renee how proud he was of her—and how grateful—and how she and Lyle would learn to love each other and were destined for joy—eventually.

He looked uncertain and anything but proud or grateful.

"What?" she asked. "What is it?"

"Two things," he told her. "First, I just got off the phone with Lyle."

Renee's stomach clenched. "What's wrong?"

Her father worked anxiously at his tie, shoved his hands deep into the pockets of his charcoal trousers, then inhaled a deep breath and let it out slowly. But he never looked at Renee once. "He, uh, he's fine. Pretty much. He's… Well, that is… I mean, it would appear…"

"Daddy, just tell me."

Reginald Riley sighed, with impatience. "Lyle called me from his car phone. He's on his way to the airport."

Renee narrowed her eyes. "The airport? What for?"

Her father ran a hand over his thinning hair. "Remember the business deal he was working on last week? The one in Hong Kong?"

How could she forget? Lyle had missed out on most of the wedding preparation because of it. "Yes. I remember."

"Well, honey, it, uh… It's gone sour on him. He has to be in Hong Kong by tonight or he could lose millions of dollars."

"What?" Renee exclaimed, a bubble of laughter escaping. "He's dumping our wedding to see to a business deal?"

Her father held his hands out in front of him, palms flat, as if he were trying to ward off a blow. "I know, honey. I told him he should be ashamed of himself, postponing his wedding this way, but—"

"Postponing?" Renee interrupted. That wasn't what she had in mind at all. She was thinking more along the lines of a total cancellation. In spite of that, she heard herself asking, "Until when?"

Reginald's gaze began to ricochet again. "He, uh… He said you two could reschedule it for later this year. He thinks early October will be good. He has to check his calendar for sure, though. He said to tell you he'd call you when he got back from Hong Kong, probably at the end of next week, and the two of you could discuss it.''

''Oh, I don't think we'll need to discuss it,'' she said. A flutter of delight tickled her stomach, and she suddenly felt lighter than air. ''Because we won't be postponing the wedding.''

''Well, I don't see how you can avoid it, since he's halfway to the airport by now.'' Her father braved a glance in her direction but quickly looked away. Then, apparently unable to believe he'd seen what he'd seen, he quickly looked back. ''Renee, honey?'' he said. ''Why are you smiling?''

Smiling? Renee thought. Hey, she was about to burst into song. However, since she knew she couldn't carry a tune, she burst into laughter instead. Nervous, anxious, but very, very happy laughter.

''You know,'' she managed to say through her giggles, ''I probably should have seen this coming from a mile away.''

Her father eyed her warily. ''You seem to be taking this awfully well.''

She laughed some more. ''Yeah, well, I think maybe the fates have been on my side on this one.''

''What are you talking about?''

''I mean I was just sitting here wondering how to tell Lyle that I can't marry him.''

This time her father was the one to exclaim, *''What?''*

Renee shook her head, then crossed the room to take his hands in hers. ''I'm sorry, Daddy, but I just can't. I don't love him. He doesn't love me. It would never work.''

''You don't think you could grow to love him someday?''

She shook her head.

''How can you be so certain?''

She smiled again. ''Because I'm in love with someone else, that's how.''

Her father's lips parted in surprise, then, just as quickly, he closed his mouth and nodded. ''That would probably explain the second thing I came in here to tell you,'' he said.

''What's that?''

''There's a man here to see you.''

Renee's heart leaped into her throat at the announcement. "What man?" she asked, her voice barely audible.

"It's one of those Fortune kids. I never can keep them all straight."

Renee swallowed hard. "Tell him to come on up."

But instead of going to do that, her father tightened his grip on her hands and met her gaze levelly. "Renee," he said, "all you had to do was tell me. I never would have asked you to marry Lyle if I'd known you were in love with someone else."

"I didn't know I was in love with someone else," she told him. "Not until I met him." Then she remembered what all this meant for her father. "But Daddy, the company. What will you do about Riley Communications?"

He shrugged philosophically. "I built one company from the ground up. Nobody says I can't do it again."

"But—"

"It's not important, Renee," he said with more conviction than she'd ever heard in his voice. "You're what's important. Your happiness. I never should have asked you to consider Lyle's proposal."

"But—"

"It'll all work out," he said. "Trust me."

She stood on tiptoe to kiss his cheek, then murmured a soft thank-you as she moved away.

After a final squeeze of her fingers, her father released her hands and made his way to the door. "I'll send the Fortune kid up on my way out."

Renee smiled when she noted her father's wording. As far as she was concerned, Garrett wasn't a kid in any way, shape or form. Then her father's statement hit her. "Where are you going?" she asked.

"To see Lyle's parents. To tell them that, even though he's worth millions, he's not nearly good enough for my little girl."

"Daddy!" she exclaimed.

He laughed softly. "Well, he's not good enough for you. Because he doesn't love you. But I promise to tell his parents that in the nicest possible way, I assure you."

She shook her head as he left, but she didn't have time to think about all he had said. Because within moments, Garrett was pushing open her bedroom door, looking gorgeous and sexy and wonderful in faded blue jeans and an even more faded denim work shirt.

"I'm sorry," he said as he entered, seeming to read her thoughts. "I left the Final Destination in a hurry this morning. I didn't have time to get myself dressed up."

This morning? He must have left at the crack of dawn.

"I flew myself here," he said, still evidently noting the train of her thoughts. "I guess I forgot to tell you that I'm a licensed pilot. In fact, there are a lot of things I forgot to tell you."

Renee's heart began to pound more furiously. "Like what?" she asked, the question barely audible in the nearly silent room. "Why did you come here?"

Garrett hesitated before responding, his gaze roving over her hungrily, taking in all her wedding finery. When he focused on her face again, his eyes were lit with something hot and anxious. And his voice came out a little rough when he told her, "Because I had to see you before you got married, that's why. I had to tell you something. Something very important."

"What?"

He swallowed hard. "Don't do it," he said.

"What?" she gasped.

"Don't do it, Renee. Don't marry Lyle Norton. Marry me instead."

At that, her heart seemed to stop beating completely. Then, just as quickly, it began to race triple time. "Wh-why would I marry you?" she managed to stammer, amazed that she asked such a thing. This was what she wanted, after all, she reminded herself, to marry Garrett. Still, she'd just canceled a wedding because she couldn't go through with a loveless marriage. Why hurry into one that would be founded on a one-sided love?

Garrett took a few tentative steps forward, stopping within inches of Renee. But instead of reaching for her, he hooked his hands on his hips and leveled a steady gaze upon her face. "Because you love me, that's why. Me, not my money."

It was a statement, not a question, indicating he was completely convinced of the fact. Renee didn't know what had changed his ideas about her in that respect, but he evidently knew she was capable of falling in love with him for some reason other than his money. Still, just because his opinion had changed didn't necessarily mean his feelings for her had.

So she told him, "Just because I love you, that's not a good enough reason to marry you. There are a lot of other things to consider."

He took another step forward, and this time he did reach for her. He cupped his hands over her shoulders, curling his fingers possessively into the billowing lace of her dress. "All right," he said. "Then do it because I love you, too."

Something squeezed Renee's lungs tight, expelling every bit of air until she began to grow dizzy. "And just how, exactly, did you come to this conclusion?" she asked. "Last I heard, you thought I was a gold-digging opportunist. What suddenly changed your mind?"

He smiled, lifting a hand to brush the backs of his bent knuckles lightly over her cheek. "You did, sweetheart. The night you let me be your first. Your only."

Renee inhaled a deep, shaky breath. "Then why didn't you say something the morning after?"

"I didn't know what to say then," he told her. "I was so confused about what had happened, I couldn't think straight. I didn't realize how I felt because I was fighting it so hard. So I didn't say anything. Then, when I woke up in the middle of the night last night, all I could think about was how you'd be getting married today, and—"

"How did you know the wedding was today?" she asked. "I never gave you a specific date."

He hesitated before confessing, "Aunt Kate told me. She called me last night to tell me how stupid I was being. And…" He lifted his other hand, framing her face. "And she told me the real reason you were marrying Lyle Norton. Because of your father. Because you felt like you owed him. Because you love him. And I got to thinking that maybe, if you loved me, too, you might call the wedding off. This wedding, I mean,'' he added with an uncertain smile. ''I don't mind if you plan another one. As long as I get to be the groom. And sweetheart, I can help your father out if all he needs is a loan. I've made some good investments. Riley Communications sounds like it might be worth looking into.''

She smiled, reaching up to circle his wrists with loose fingers. ''I'll tell Daddy. But Garrett, don't worry about the wedding. There's not going to be one today.''

He released his breath in a long rush of obvious relief. ''You called it off?''

She shook her head. ''Actually, Lyle did.''

Garrett's smile fell. ''Oh. Then you didn't—''

''But Lyle only wanted to postpone it.'' She hastened to clarify things. ''I'm the one who canceled it.''

His smile returned. ''Oh,'' he repeated more lightheartedly. ''Then that means you're a bride without a groom at the moment.''

''Oh, no, I'm not,'' she said. ''I have my groom right here. And I'm not letting him out of my sight until we're husband and wife.''

''Then you'll marry me?''

She nodded. ''You bet I'll marry you.''

Without thinking, Renee pushed herself on tiptoe and covered Garrett's mouth with hers. Goodness, but the man made her feel bold. This was the second time she'd set her mind to seducing him. Before, she hadn't been certain of the response she would receive from him. This time she didn't have the slightest doubt. Garrett was hers for the taking.

Forever.

So she took him, heart, body and soul. Just curled her fingers into his hair and pulled his head closer to hers, rolling her tongue into his mouth when he parted his lips in surprise.

As quickly as that surprise surfaced, though, Garrett tamped it down, roping his arms around Renee's waist to tug her off the ground and into his embrace. Without hesitation, he made his way to her bed, settling her onto it, following her down.

Renee toed off her white slippers as she went, then reached for her veil and wrestled it off, tossing it unheeded to the floor.

"Help me get this dress off," she said. "I suddenly find it to be a huge burden."

She didn't have to ask him twice. Garrett turned her until her back was to him, then made short work of the long row of satin buttons that spanned her back from neck to waist. The moment he'd freed the last one, Renee pulled the garment from her shoulders and down her arms, tossing it, too, into a neglected heap on the floor.

"Hey, you better take care of that," Garrett said. "You're going to be needing it for our wedding."

She shook her head. "No, I won't. That dress was and is totally inappropriate. For our wedding, I just want something simple and innocent, something classic and everlasting. Like my love for you. And I want to be married at the Final Destination," she said. "Maybe in that field of clover where we got caught in the rain that day. And I know the perfect wedding planner for the job. Your cousin Chloe told me she hired Mollie Shaw to plan her and Mason's wedding. Mollie did Mac and Kelly's, too, and I think she'd be perfect for ours. We'll just keep it all in the family that way."

But Garrett was only half listening to what Renee was saying. Because his gaze—along with nearly every scrap of his attention—was focused instead on what she was—almost—wearing beneath her wedding dress.

When he realized she had stopped talking, he said in a soft whisper, "I can't believe this is what you were going to wear for Lyle."

At first she didn't answer him, and something inside Garrett tightened fiercely. When he looked at her face, however, that tautness immediately eased. Because what he saw in Renee's eyes reassured him that there had never been anyone but him, that there never would be anyone but him.

"I never planned to wear this for Lyle," she told him softly. "The whole time I was getting dressed this morning, I was thinking about you, Garrett. I never could have gone through with my wedding to Lyle. Not after you and I made love. Not after I fell in love with you the way I did. I was only kidding myself about my feelings for him. For you, though…''

''What?'' he asked.

''My love is true blue,'' she said.

An urgency swept over Garrett when he saw the look in her eyes. ''Renee, honey,'' he began, ''I know I said that if I had a second chance to make love to you I'd take it slow and easy and all, but I want you something fierce right now, so what I was wondering is, since we have the rest of our lives together to make slow, leisurely love, would you mind too much if we didn't go slow this time? It's just that—''

She cut him off with a kiss reminiscent of a tsunami, rolling their bodies until she was straddling him, nearly consuming him. Garrett figured that pretty much qualified as agreement, so he fell onto the mattress easily, pulling Renee closer as he did, tugging on her white teddy the moment the two of them were prone. She helped as much as she could by wriggling out of it, and Garrett did his part when he located the three snaps between her legs and freed those. He pushed the silky fabric around her waist just as she pushed it down. And as she sat astride him with the wisp of white bunched around her middle, Garrett moved his hands to her naked bottom, cupping her possessively in both hands, settling a finger lightly in the cleft that divided her.

Renee uttered a soft cry of pleasure at his errant touch, moving herself languidly backward in silent encouragement for more. When she did, the moist, heated heart of her rubbed against the rough denim of his shirt, and she gasped with pleasure at the sensation. Then she moved forward again. Then back. Then forward. Garrett sucked in a breath when he realized what she was doing. With one hand still curving over her derriere, he wrapped the fingers of his other around her wrist. Then he urged her hand between their bodies to the buttons of his shirt.

''I want to feel your skin on mine,'' he said huskily. ''Hot. Naked. Needy.''

She uttered another low, lascivious sound, then went about unbuttoning his shirt. Quickly, deftly, they made short work of his confining garments, then returned to their original position. Although Renee had shed her teddy, her garter belt still rode low on her naked hips, her silky stockings rubbing along the tender skin of Garrett's ribs. As she moved over his flat belly, she was hot and damp against him. Garrett groaned out his need for her, but when she reached for the garters to unfasten her stockings, he closed his fingers over hers.

"Don't," he said with a wicked, wicked grin. "I've always had a fantasy about making love to a woman wearing nothing but stockings and a garter belt."

She flushed from her cheeks to her breasts. "You mean you never have before?" she asked.

He shook his head.

"So this will be your first time?"

He smiled, nodding slowly.

"Well, then, Garrett," she said, moving slowly, slickly over his torso again, expelling a shuddering breath as she went, "I guess I'll be your first, won't I? But don't worry. I'll be gentle with you."

Contrary to her assurance, however, Renee was like a tigress when she moved on him again. Garrett reached up to fill his hands with her breasts, rubbing his thumbs over the stiff peaks, circling her nipples with sure fingers before pulling her down to his mouth. Renee arched against him as she came down, then gasped when he covered one breast and tugged hard, laving her with the flat of his tongue. But when he moved to take her other breast into his hungry mouth, she pulled back.

"What?" he asked.

"I want to touch you this time," she said. "I didn't get to last time."

Before he could say a word, she straightened and reached behind herself, covering as much of his stiff shaft as she could take in both hands. Her eyes widened when she realized how big he was, but she deftly skimmed her fingers upward, over the top of him, then down to the base again.

"Oh, Garrett," she murmured. "You're so…oh."

Over and over she lifted and lowered her hands, creating a friction against him that drove him to the erotic edge. The feel of her fingers against him and the sight of her arching above him, totally uninhibited, totally vulnerable, totally his, were almost more than he could bear. Grasping her hips tightly, he pulled her above his body and pushed her back, spearing her, penetrating her before either of them realized his intention.

And then he was filling her slick channel, up, up, up inside her, joining them together in a perfect union. He paused for only a moment, long enough for her to become accustomed to his invasion, long enough to feel how wonderful, how right the joining was. Then, as she opened her eyes and met his gaze with a languid smile, Garrett jerked his hips upward, launching himself in and out of her with an even, measured movement.

Immediately, Renee caught his rhythm and joined in. Heat filled Garrett as he watched her, and time evaporated into nothing. Little by little the tension between them built, and little by little he gladly lost himself to her. And when Renee's breathing began to increase, Garrett quickened his pace to go with her. A white-hot explosion rocked him as he emptied himself inside her, and he rolled their bodies until she lay beneath him so that he could fill her more completely and carry her home, too. Immediately, she cried out her completion, clinging to Garrett as he clung to her—totally, irrevocably.

For a long time they lay entwined, gasping for breath, groping for coherent thought, enjoying the satisfaction of having found such a perfect love. And when Renee turned her head to gaze at him, she smiled the kind of smile he knew he'd see for the rest of his life. A smile of love. Of truth. Of commitment.

And he knew then that both of them had found the Right Thing.

Epilogue

"It was a beautiful wedding, Renee."

Renee turned to smile at Garrett's cousin Chloe, who sat perched on the countertop in the Final Destination's kitchen. "Thanks," she said. "But I can't take credit for it. I couldn't have had my June wedding without Mollie. Thanks for recommending her."

"Hey, thank Kelly," Chloe said, tucking a length of honey blond hair behind one ear. "She's the one who started this chain reaction of weddings that seems to be taking place among the Fortune ranks. I only hope Mollie's not exhausted by the time she gets to my and Mason's wedding. Then again, maybe *exhausted* would be the right theme for ours."

Renee narrowed her eyes at Chloe's tone. Funny, but she didn't sound all that thrilled about her upcoming wedding. "What are you talking about?" she asked. "Is everything okay between you and Mason?"

"Great," Chloe said dryly. "Just great. He handles me with kid gloves. Damn him."

Renee chuckled. "He's just a decent guy, that's all," she said. "A total gentleman."

"A little *too* decent and gentlemanly sometimes if you ask me," Chloe said sullenly. "I wish he'd be as attentive to me as Garrett is to you. You two look so happy together."

Renee smiled. "That's because we *are* happy together."

Chloe nodded. "Good. You deserve it. So you guys are going to stay here in Wyoming, huh?"

"Yep. We're going to make the Final Destination a viable cattle ranch. Garrett's resigned from his position at Fortune, and he's got everything under control here. It feels good to be working together this way. It feels right."

Chloe nodded her approval. "That's exactly as it should be. I just wish I could say the same about me and Mason."

Before Renee could comment on that odd statement—Chloe and Mason were perfect for each other, after all—and as if roused by the women's conversation, Garrett and Mason Chandler pushed through the kitchen door engaged in lively conversation.

"I'm telling you, Garrett," Mason said, clearly agitated about something, "this could potentially be very serious."

"I'm not disagreeing with you, Mase," Garrett returned. But his attention obviously wasn't on the dialogue he was sharing with Chloe's fiancé. Instead, his gaze was focused entirely on Renee.

She felt the heat of that gaze right down to her soul and wished the wedding reception would hurry up and come to an end so the two of them could be alone together. He looked so handsome in his dark, Western-cut suit, the attire a perfect complement to Renee's simple, sleeveless ivory sheath. The bright June sunshine spilled through the kitchen window near him, gilding his hair with gold and brightening his tawny eyes. But before she could say a word, Mason Chandler began to speak again.

"Someone's been buying up stock in Stuart's company for some time now, but I haven't been able to figure out exactly who. Signs point to Gray McGuire—"

"Gray McGuire?" Garrett echoed. "What interest would he have in my father's business?"

"I don't know yet," Mason told him. "That's the problem. But it looks like he's the one. And I intend to find out what's behind his interest."

Garrett shook his head and sighed with impatience. "Mase, you just seem to know everything about everybody. Why is that?"

A shutter fell over Mason's face, erasing any sign of what he might be feeling. "I'm just a knowledgeable guy, okay? And I'm telling you, if McGuire is behind this, then he's up to no good. You better tell Stuart to keep his eyes open."

"My father can take care of his own business interests, Mase," Garrett assured the other man. "Don't worry about it so much."

Mason opened his mouth to say more, but Chloe cut him off.

"That's our signal to head out," she told her fiancé, jumping from the countertop, tugging at Mason's sleeve. Before she left, however, she stood on tiptoe to kiss Garrett briefly on the cheek. "Congratulations," she said. "I'm happy you found the real thing."

"Me, too," Garrett replied. He spoke the words not to Chloe, but to Renee. "Me, too."

He waited until the couple had left, then made his way to Renee. "Come on out to the reception," he said. "Let Mollie take care of all this stuff."

"I just wanted to make sure there was plenty of champagne," she said.

He tugged her into his arms and pressed his lips lightly to her temple. "Planning on making this a long celebration, Mrs. Fortune?"

She nodded as she wrapped her arms around his waist. "A lifetime celebration, Mr. Fortune."

He inhaled deeply, and she felt his heartbeat slow against hers, his utter contentment clear in the embrace. "Then grab a bottle and let's get rid of all these people."

She chuckled low. "These people are family," she reminded him.

"Then they won't be offended when we tell them all to scram."

She shook her head slowly, but couldn't quite bring herself to disagree. "Okay. You take the Fortunes, I'll take the Rileys. Together, we should be able to clear this place out pretty quickly."

He smiled as he held her at arm's length. "Together," he echoed. "I do like the sound of that word."

Renee wiggled her eyebrows playfully. "Then you just wait to see what else I have planned for us to do together," she told him.

"Why, Mrs. Fortune," he said. "I do believe you're trying to seduce me."

"Yes, well, seeing as how I'm two for two in that respect, you'll forgive me if I consider you a total pushover."

"Sweetheart," he said as he curled an arm around her waist and steered her out the kitchen door, "you can push me over anytime at all. Just don't expect to be getting up again too soon when you do."

Together they laughed as they exited the kitchen, and together they made their way to the guests milling about outside the house. Together, they brought the reception to a quick conclusion, and together they left for their honeymoon destination, the little cabin out back that Kate Fortune had given them for a wedding present.

And as Renee linked her hand with Garrett's, she couldn't help but turn and search for his aunt among the guests. She found Kate quickly, gazing right at the two of them, a knowing smile curling her lips. Renee smiled as she held up her hand in silent farewell and thanks. Kate lifted her fingers to her lips for a moment before tossing the two of them a benediction in return.

All was well at the Final Destination, Renee thought as she and Garrett made their way to the cabin. More than that, all was right.

*　*　*　*　*

*Find out what happens to Amanda Corbain
when all of a sudden she's living under the same
roof as her boss in*

The Secretary and the Millionaire
by
Leanne Banks

For a sneak preview turn the page...

"Amanda, I need you *now*."

Jack Fortune's words on Amanda Corbain's intercom kicked her heart into overdrive. She'd never heard that tone from him, and never coupled with those exact words—except in her dreams. "I'll be right there," she managed, and swiveled out of her chair.

She opened his office door to find him pacing, his long stride covering the generous width of his office. He stopped when she closed the door behind her.

"It's the housekeeper's day off. The nanny is sick," he told Amanda as he raked his hand through his hair, "and I'm closing the Eastco deal today."

He walked toward her, and her stomach dipped. For Amanda, stomach dips, butterflies and accelerated heartbeats had become part and parcel of working for Jack. The challenge lay in not letting her feelings show.

"This isn't part of your job description, but I need someone I can count on to take care of Lilly now. Today. Will you do it?"

"Of course," she said, then gave a light laugh. He truly had no idea of all that she would do for him. "I thought you were going to ask something difficult."

He exhaled in relief and shook his head. "You're one hell of an assistant, Amanda. You can be sure I'll remember this at your next performance review," he told her.

Amanda felt a twinge at his professional tone. "That's not necessary. My experience taking care of my brother and sisters doesn't have much to do with my office performance."

"No. But in this case, it does with *mine*. I should warn you Lilly still hasn't adjusted to living with me."

"That's understandable," Amanda said, the slight nervousness in his voice surprising her and grabbing at her heart. "Her mother hasn't been gone very long. That will change."

"God, I hope so," he muttered, returning to his desk. "The poor kid hides behind the furniture every time I enter the room. The nanny I hired has impeccable references, but Lilly hasn't warmed to her." He frowned, then seemed to switch gears. "Use one of the company limos. As soon as the meeting is over, I'll come home."

Amanda nodded, hesitating before she said, "You asked me to remind you about your dinner date with Ms. Sullivan."

He frowned. "I'll cancel."

Amanda wrestled with her conscience. Trina Sullivan, a beautiful redhead, was Jack's current social partner. She swallowed her reluctance and envy in one gulp. "You don't have to cancel. I'll stay with Lilly tonight."

He shook his head. "No. I'll cancel."

Amanda bit her tongue to keep from screaming with joy.

Thirty-five minutes later the nanny, pale and clearly ill, invited Amanda into the marble foyer, introduced her to Lilly, then disappeared to her upstairs bedroom.

Amanda looked down at the perfectly dressed three-year-old, gripping a worn, stuffed one-eyed cat. Lilly's blond hair fell past her shoulders in tousled curls. The sorrow in her wide green eyes made Amanda's heart turn over.

She knelt in front of Lilly. "I have a cat, too. Her name is Delilah. What's your cat's name?"

"Miss Annabelle," Lilly whispered.

Amanda's heart twisted at the fear on her face. Lilly seemed such a tiny forlorn figure, especially in the grand surroundings of Jack's home. "You wanna go outside for a while?"

Lilly nodded, and when Jack's daughter put her tiny hand in Amanda's, Amanda's heart was lost.

* * *

Don't forget The Secretary and the Millionaire
is on the shelves now!

*Welcome back to the drama
and mystery that is the
Fortune Dynasty.*

 *A Fortune's Children Wedding* is
coming to you at a special
price of only £3.99 and
contains a money off coupon for issue one
of *Fortune's Children Brides*.

With issue one priced at a
special introductory offer
of 99p you can get it
FREE with your money
off coupon.

Published 24 March 2000

Published 21 April 2000

Published 19 May 2000

Available at most branches of WH Smith, Tesco, Tesco Ireland, Martins, RS McCall, Forbuoys, Borders, Easons, and other leading bookshops

▼™ SILHOUETTE
SPECIAL EDITION ®

AVAILABLE FROM 19TH MAY 2000

SHE'S HAVING HIS BABY Linda Randall Wisdom

That's My Baby!

Jake Roberts was everything Caitlin O'Hara wanted in her baby's father—he was fun, warm and gorgeous. They'd shared every intimate detail of their lives since childhood. Why not a baby?

A FATHER'S VOW Myrna Temte

Montana

Sam Brightwater wanted to start a traditional family. So the *last* woman he should be attracted to was Julia Stedman, who was only sampling her heritage. But Julia got under his skin and soon they were making love and making a baby…

BETH AND THE BACHELOR Susan Mallery

Beth was a suburban mother of two and her friends had set her up with a blind date—millionaire bachelor Todd Graham! He was sexy, eligible—everything a woman could want…

BUCHANAN'S PRIDE Pamela Toth

Leah Randall took in the man without a memory, but she had no idea who he was. They never planned to fall in love, not when he could be anyone…even one of her powerful Buchanan neighbours!

THE LONG WAY HOME Cheryl Reavis

Rita Warren had come home. She had things to prove. She didn't need a troublemaking soldier in her already complicated life. But 'Mac' McGraw was just impossible to ignore.

CHILD MOST WANTED Carole Halston

Susan Gulley had become a mother to her precious orphaned nephew, but she hadn't banked on falling for his handsome but hard-edged uncle. What would Jonah do when he learned the secret she'd been keeping?

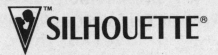

Sometimes bringing up baby can bring surprises —and showers of love! For the cutest and cuddliest heroes and heroines, choose the Special Edition™ book marked

That's my baby!

SILHOUETTE
SPECIAL EDITION®

TMB/RTL1